MW01165300

Friendship

Other titles in the series Life—A How-to Guide

Choosing a Community Service Career
A How-to Guide
Library ed. 978-1-59845-147-4
Paperback 978-1-59845-312-6

Dealing With Stress
A How-to Guide
Library ed. 978-0-7660-3439-6
Paperback 978-1-59845-309-6

Volunteering
A How-to Guide
Library ed. 978-0-7660-3440-2
Paperback 978-1-59845-310-2

Getting the Hang of Fashion and Dress Codes
A How-to Guide
Library ed. 978-0-7660-3444-0
Paperback 978-1-59845-313-3

Getting Ready to Drive
A How-to Guide
Library ed. 978-0-7660-3443-3
Paperback 978-1-59845-314-0

Using Technology
A How-to Guide
Library ed. 978-0-7660-3441-9
Paperback 978-1-59845-311-9

Friendship

A How-to Guide

Life
A How-to Guide

Jan Burns

Enslow Publishers, Inc.
40 Industrial Road
Box 398
Berkeley Heights, NJ 07922
USA

http://www.enslow.com

Library of Congress Cataloging-in-Publication Data

Burns, Jan.
  Friendship : a how-to guide / Jan Burns.
    p. cm.—(Life—a how-to guide)
  Includes bibliographical references and index.
  Summary: "Find out how to make and keep friends, cliques, popularity, online friends and communication, teen guys and girls, attitude, and ending friendships"—Provided by publisher.
  ISBN 978-0-7660-3442-6
  1. Friendship—Juvenile literature. I. Title.
  BF575.F66B87 2011
  158.2'5—dc22
                              2010033038

Paperback ISBN 978-1-59845-315-7

Printed in the United States of America

072011 Lake Book Manufacturing, Inc., Melrose Park, IL

10 9 8 7 6 5 4 3 2 1

To Our Readers: We have done our best to make sure all Internet addresses in this book were active and appropriate when we went to press. However, the author and the publisher have no control over and assume no liability for the material available on those Internet sites or on other Web sites they may link to. Any comments or suggestions can be sent by e-mail to comments@enslow.com or to the address on the back cover.

♻ Enslow Publishers, Inc., is committed to printing our books on recycled paper. The paper in every book contains 10% to 30% post-consumer waste (PCW). The cover board on the outside of each book contains 100% PCW. Our goal is to do our part to help young people and the environment too!

Illustration Credits: All clipart © 2011 Clipart.com, a division of Getty Images. All rights reserved.; BananaStock, pp. 20, 33, 99; Corbis Images Royalty-Free, pp. 22, 82, 96; Digital Vision, p. 6; Eyewire Images, p. 29; © 2011 Photos.com, a division of Getty Images. All rights reserved., pp. 11, 14, 47, 51, 57, 68, 73, 80, 84, 87, 91, 106, 111, 114; Shutterstock.com, pp. 1, 3, 16, 25, 36, 38, 43, 64, 77.

Cover Illustration: Shutterstock.com (six smiling teens).

Contents

1 Friendship 7

2 Popularity 22

3 Cliques 38

4 Online Friendships and Communication 51

5 Making Friends 66

6 Teen Guys and Girls 82

7 Attitude 99

Chapter Notes 115

Glossary 124

Further Reading and
Internet Addresses 125

Index 126

Friendships fill a deep need
we all have to be accepted.

Friendship

The first Sunday in August was proclaimed National Friendship Day by the United States Congress in 1935.

**"Friends give us a sense of belonging,"
says fifteen-year-old Melissa.** "We all have that moment where we walk into a party and feel like we don't know anyone. Or, we walk into the cafeteria on the first day of school and wonder where to sit. Then, we see a friend and a rush of relief washes over us. We know where to go."[1]

Kids say that life without friends would be hard. It could get really lonely and rather boring. Who would cheer you up when you've had a bad day? Who would listen to you when you talk about all your hopes and dreams? Only your friends will do. Each one is different, and each one helps you in his or her own unique way.

Good friends can be counted on to stick by you through all the challenges and triumphs that life sometimes brings. They are the ones you just can't wait to talk to each day. What could be better than that?

Years later, you will remember all the crazy and wonderful things you did together and be thankful you have those great memories. There will probably also be a few sad ones, but that is part of life, too. You just have to learn from them and move on.

Importance of Friendships

Friendships play a very important part in young people's lives as they grow up. They fill a deep need that human beings have to be accepted. Friends help teens laugh and have fun. They can talk together, plan adventures, and share memories, some of which they will never forget.

Quiz: How Well Do You Know Your Friends?

1. What do they like on their pizza?
2. What are their favorite subjects in school?
3. What are their middle names?
4. What kind of pets do they have?
5. What do they want to be when they grow up?

"As teens emotionally distance themselves from their parents and become more independent, good friends provide the emotional support and nurturing they still need," says clinical psychologist Patricia Wills.[2]

Friends may be even more important than was previously believed. According to the National Center for Health Education, friendships are as vital to health as maintaining a proper diet.[3]

According to some psychologists, friendships provide people with companionship, stimulation, physical support, support if you're feeling down, and true affection.[4]

The Great Things About Friends

Having friends can help you handle tough times. You can talk about what you are going through and ask for advice. By the time you are a teen, there are some things you don't want to discuss with your parents. That is normal. That's where your friends come in. They may be experiencing some of the same things you are, so they understand what you are going through. Just talking to a friend often will make you feel better. You will feel less alone and less vulnerable.

Good friends make you feel safe. You can act silly with them, and they won't think you're weird. You can also share your worries. They will be sure to give you feedback and advice. Some of it may be encouraging. Some of it may make you think twice. But that's good. It may stop you from making a mistake.

"I can bring my problems to my friends," says fifteen-year-old Matt. "And when something good happens, you want to tell them that, too."[5]

In her book *Be True to Yourself*, Amanda Ford looks back on her teen years and says, "There is nothing like having close girl friends. It is wonderful to have girls you can go to parties with, or cry to when you are feeling upset. You grow together and learn from each other's experiences."[6]

You can learn a lot from your friends. They bring their own knowledge, personalities, and life stories to the friendship. When you share your life with them, it can help all of you to learn new things, to change, and to grow. Writer Julie Taylor says that your friends are "more precious than diamonds or gold and they should be treated as such."[7]

"A lot of times in high school people don't necessarily like their friends. They just hang out with them because they're afraid of being alone. Or, they want to be with the popular crowd. But one really good friend is worth a dozen superficial ones," says actress Anne Hathaway.[8]

Lots of Variety

You may have all different kinds of friends in your life. Some are probably more like acquaintances because you don't know them very well. You may just say "hi" to them when you pass them in the halls at school. Others are true friends who are like members of your family.

Good friends can be counted on to stick with you through life's challenges and help you celebrate the good times.

Do you have one friend in particular whom you call when you feel like doing something? Maybe you are like sixteen-year-old Jamie, who says, "I have a ton of friends, but none of them are more fun than Katie is. There's never a dull moment with her around. When I'm with her, I feel like I'm in a movie or something."[9]

With some friends, you may feel as if you've known them forever, as thirteen-year-old Tamara says about her friend. "I've known Kelly since kindergarten. She was there when I lost my first tooth. . . . When my parents got divorced, I felt like everything in my world was changing. But when I was with Kelly, I felt okay again because she is a constant source of support and always has been."[10]

Or you might have some friends you just met and are still getting to know. That's cool, too. You can look forward to sharing stories, having fun, and enjoying their friendship.

Just for Fun

Make a list of all the fun things you do with your friends. Your list might include such things as going to the movies, shopping, listening to music, or going to the beach. Then, make a list of things that would be fun to do in the future—going to a concert, taking a road trip, or going to a baseball or basketball game. Be creative. Think up some new exciting plans so you will always have things to look forward to.

What Is a Good Friend?

Everyone has a different idea about what makes a good friend. These are some of the ways that teens describe a friend:

- Someone you can always trust.

- Someone who is always there when you need him or her.

- Someone who will tell you the truth.

- Someone who will talk with you about your problems or come to you with his or hers.

- Someone who won't encourage you to do something that is dangerous.[11]

"My mother once told me about a saying in Spanish that describes friendship: '*Mis amigos son las personas con las que me entiendo.*' Translated it means: 'Friendship is a place where I can understand myself with someone else,'" says Colin.[12]

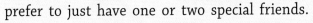

People have different needs for friends. Some people are much more comfortable doing things in groups. Others, however, prefer to just have one or two special friends. No one can tell you how many friends you should have. That's up to you to decide.

There are plusses and minuses about having a large group of friends. It can be hard sometimes to get along with so many different people. Also, it can be difficult to get everyone to agree on something—a movie or a barbecue, or should we just order pizza? However, on the plus side, it's nice to know there's usually someone to call when you want to do something.

Best Friends

Do you have a best friend? You have probably read books or have seen other TV shows and movies that have featured best friendships. For example, in the Harry Potter books, Harry, Hermione, and Ron have all risked their lives for each other many times. You can't get closer than that.

Some people say a best friend is like the sister or brother they never had.

A best friend is probably someone you think is special, who likes many of the same things that you do, and who is fun to be around. He or she probably feels the same way about you, too.

"My best friend and I do everything together. She's like the sister I never had. She knows exactly what I'm going to say before I even say it. We're so on the same wavelength, it's almost scary. When we're together, I feel like I can conquer the world. I would do absolutely anything for that girl," says Joni.[13]

Studies show that only about one-third of kids in high school have a best friend.[14] If you are one of the two-thirds of these teens who don't have one, it might be that you haven't met the right person to be your best friend. Or it could be that you would rather have a lot of friends instead of just concentrating on one person. Some people tend to be closer to family members, such as sisters and brothers, than to people outside the family. You can't force best friendships. They usually develop over a long period of time, and they either happen or they don't.

Best friendships may be challenged as teens change as they get older. One male teen had a best friend, but eventually he felt he needed more breathing room from that person. "We were like Tweedledee and Tweedledum—it was cool, but it was also a little stuffy in there. We're still friends, though."[15]

Teen Troubles

Below are some problems or challenges teens said they have faced with the help of a friend:

- Not making a soccer or basketball team
- Being dumped by a boyfriend or girlfriend
- Learning that their parents are getting a divorce
- A serious health problem, such as cancer, in themselves or a relative[16]

Besides this, not all friendships are created equal. Some may be strong enough to last for years. Others, however, might only last while you're in the same class at school or on the same team. This is because people change and develop different interests over time. This has a direct effect on friendships.

A friend can help you feel better by listening and giving you a new perspective.

According to psychologist Marlin Potash, "You can outgrow friends the same way you outgrow clothes and haircuts—you get older, you change, and you move on to new experiences."[17]

Friends Help Friends

Have you ever made a mistake or had something bad happen and then told a friend about it? Your friend probably tried to make you feel better, maybe by reminding you that you have survived problems before. Or he or she may have told you that the world wasn't really ending. He or she may have also tried to find something positive in the situation.

"Friends help you stay on the right path," says Steven. "No matter what, they understand and accept all your changes as you grow into young adults."[18]

Friends build up each other's self-images. If you are feeling low because you didn't do well on a test or your parents just told you that you couldn't get something you had really wanted, a friend can help you see other sides of the situation. They may even be able to get you to laugh at yourself. These are some of the benefits of friendships.

If you have a friend who is going through a tough time, don't let him or her down. Be there, even if it is only to listen. The important thing is that friends know you are there for them.

Try to think of things that might help your friend to feel better. Talk over possible solutions. He or she will appreciate it, and you will feel good about yourself for trying to help.

Arguments

Sometimes, even with good friends, you may have arguments or misunderstandings. That's human nature. If that happens, don't keep your feelings bottled up inside until they explode. Instead, have a talk and tell your friend how you feel. Be specific. Don't accuse him or her of "always" doing something or "never" doing something. Be sure to let your friend give his or her side of the story, too.

If you ask teens what their arguments are about, they will tell you it was often over something small. Thirteen-year-old Nick says, "My buddy Neil and I had a big fight about something incredibly stupid. I don't even know how it started, but it kept going on, and things were said and more things, and our friends got in the middle, and now we hate each other. I still feel bad."[19]

If your friend apologizes, forgive him or her and move on. Or, if the situation is reversed, maybe you should apologize. Remember that people do not always agree. The important

Five Ways to Be a Great Friend

- Be the kind of person whom people want to be around.
- Do things to make your friends feel special.
- Be a good listener.
- Talk to your friends about things that interest them.
- Be honest. Friends don't lie to each other.

thing is how you resolve your differences. Teens who have done that successfully say that afterward they felt closer because they shared their feelings and learned a little bit more about each other.

After an argument, it may take some time before you and your friend can totally rebuild the bond of trust that goes with friendship. But, with some time and communication on both sides, it can be done.

> **O**ne definition of a friend— a person who cares deeply about you and shows it.

Dealing With Disappointments

In friendships there can also be times when someone lets you down and disappoints you. In one of her books, writer Julie Taylor relates that when she was a teen, her friend Maura hurt her feelings deeply after her cat J.D. died. Maura laughed at Taylor for acting so "stupid" over a "dumb cat." Because of this incident, the two stopped being friends.[20]

If Maura had been a real friend, it's likely she would have known how much Taylor loved J.D. and wouldn't have made fun of her. At the very least, she wouldn't have made the comments that she did. Part of being a good friend is knowing when you shouldn't say something if it will make the situation worse. Think how your words will affect the other person before saying anything. If you do say something wrong, apologize as soon as you can.

Wrong Crowd?

You may also be let down if you become friends with a group of people whom you thought might have made good friends, but who didn't. These people may try to get you to make bad decisions with them, such as cutting classes, cheating on exams, smoking, drinking, or taking drugs. Peer pressure is something many kids go through, and it's not always easy to resist.

Even best friends have arguments and misunderstandings. Relationships can be rebuilt if both people make an effort.

If you are ever asked to do things that make you feel uncomfortable, learn the power of saying no. Whatever the situation, only agree to things that you feel good about. You don't have to give anyone reasons why you don't want to do something. Or, you could tell them that they made their own decisions and you made yours. Don't let them try to change your mind. It's your life.

As business executive Jack Welch says, "Control your own destiny, or someone else will."[21]

What Makes You Happy?

Sometimes you may think that certain things will make you happy. You may think that if you date someone popular, have lots of cool clothes, or make the team, you will be happy. But these things can change in a second. It is far more likely that the love you share with your family and friends will bring you true happiness.

"[Who's] going to comfort you when your mom dies? [Who's] going to let you cry when you go through your first breakup? Money isn't going to get you through these hard times—friends are," says one teen.[22] Having friends is important. Trust your instincts, and choose your friends for the right reasons.

Chapter 2 Popularity

Many teens say that physical attractiveness is an important part of popularity.

Popularity can have a big effect on friendships. Sometimes teens will try to be friends with other kids simply because they are popular, not because they truly want to be friends with them. This can lead to problems and challenges for all involved.

Meg Cabot, author of the best-selling *Princess Diaries* series, says, "Traveling around the country on my book tours, I hear a lot about what's on kids' minds. Popularity in school is intrinsically linked with self-image—especially among girls."[1]

What Makes a Person Popular?

If you ask teens to describe popular people, they are likely to mention a number of characteristics. For instance, they may say that popular teens wear cool clothes, have plenty of money, and are good athletes.

Looking good. Many kids say that popular teens are usually attractive. Most popular teens are also in good physical shape. That could be because they are involved in school sports or are on a drill team or cheerleading squad. Or it might be simply because they exercise a lot. Sometimes it's a matter of just having good genes. When other teens look at them, they are often envious. They want to be slender and attractive like them.

Getting along. Many popular teens also have good social skills, sometimes called people skills. They help people communicate with others. Social skills include being able to carry on a conversation, knowing when to listen, and how to answer. These teens are good at talking with people. How did they get that way? Some people are naturally gifted. It is a part of their personalities. Others may have gained these skills through being in team sports, band, or other group activities where they have to interact regularly with other people.

Studies show that when people feel good about themselves and their appearance, they project an air of confidence. This helps them when they have to make a presentation, give a speech, or run for a student-body office.

Good relationships with parents. Many popular teens also have good relationships with their parents. Instead of arguing and fighting, they talk things out. This leads to both sides feeling at ease with each other.[2]

This may come in handy when the teens ask for favors. These may include getting their own car, use of a family vehicle, the latest electronic gadgets, and money. This is not to say that every popular teen has all of these things, but many of them do. This adds to their appeal.

Part of a crowd. Popular teens are often surrounded by a crowd of other teens. Some of these people are genuine friends. Others just want to be seen with the popular teens. They may not necessarily like them.

What Teens Say About Popular Teens

1. "They care about life in general and what influence they have on others. They don't hang in a bad crowd, but try to make a difference."
2. "The people who are popular don't care about how others really feel. Everything is judged by how much it was, how it looks on you, when and where you got it, and how many you have of it."
3. "Popular kids are well known, have good attitudes toward others, and . . . dress pretty good."[3]

Friendship

Many popular teens are active in extracurricular activities, such as sports or the prom committee.

It is possible that they simply want to be where the action is, and popular teens are usually at the center of any action. One reason for this is that they usually are active in extracurricular activities at school. Records of this can be found sprinkled throughout their high-school yearbooks. They can be seen in photos for school clubs, athletics, student council, student-body officers, homecoming, and prom. Besides this, they also tend to be active outside school, as well.

Deserving popularity. By itself, being popular isn't bad. Sometimes popular teens deserve all the good things that popularity brings with it, such as lots of friends and attention. They truly represent the positive side of popularity.

These boys and girls are kind to others. They don't try to take advantage of any special favors or treatment offered by would-be friends. Many may also have a good sense of humor.

What Teens Say Makes Someone Popular

1. Danielle, eighteen, said being popular means "having a decent amount of friends that are there for you and you hang out with a lot of the time."
2. Popularity is having "as many friends as possible and to have everyone know you," says Nate.
3. "I think . . . [popularity is] nice to have, but not everyone can be popular," Alex says. "So, no, I don't really care because if I'm supposed to be popular then I will be, and if I'm not, it's nothing against me."
4. "Teens will do anything to become popular. I think they will demean themselves," says one teen.
5. Others feel there are ways for teens to gain popularity and stay true to who they are. Alex says, "Be funny, go to parties, (and) play sports. They have to have something that people look up to them for."[4]

Friendship

Writer Sara Eisen describes her popular teen friend Nikki this way, saying, "She had some light inside her body. . . . She was always noticed, always invited everywhere, always confided in, and never dissed. I never once heard that anyone was mad at her, despite all the attention she got. I don't need to tell you that is a major accomplishment in the esteemed teen population."[5]

Not so deserving. Other popular teens are not popular because they are friendly or because they have great personalities. They may be popular simply because they are good looking, have cool clothes, or have lots of money. Sometimes the attention they get makes them feel that they are better than others are. This can cause them to act stuck-up and snobbish. They may try to control other people. These teens may make fun of others because of the way they look, talk, or act.

One Teen's Story

This emphasis on popularity that teens face in school can sometimes make them think it is more important than it really is. For example, one teen was so embarrassed by not being invited to a popular teen's party that she lied when a friend asked her about it. She said she was not going to the party because she did not like the guy who was giving it. She told her friend she had other plans, but that night she stayed at home and cried. She felt rejected that she had not been invited.

However, she said she was surprised a few weeks later, when no one even remembered who was at the party and who was not. What had seemed so all-important to her earlier turned out not to be so important after all. That experience taught her not to stress so much, especially over things that she could not control.[6]

Rejection Hurts

Some teens say that when they tried to become friends with popular teens, they were pushed away. They were judged as not being cool enough. Being treated that way can hurt. It can also provoke anger and resentment.

"I always felt I was not good enough for any of them. That's the way the other girls were treating me, but that was wrong," says Mandee.[7]

This type of behavior can also be confusing. One teen asks, "Isn't the point of being popular to have friends? So, why would you want to make enemies by acting like you are too good for other girls? It's senseless."[8]

However, looking back on her popular teen years, one person offers a different explanation, saying, "Many people thought I was a snob. I wasn't a snob. I was just insecure and afraid of being rejected. I talked a lot when I was with my friends, but when I was around people I didn't know very well, I said very little. This quietness led others to believe, 'She thinks she's better than everyone else.'"[9]

This teen's experience shows that sometimes people can be wrong. They may misjudge other teens. What they think is snobbishness may really be insecurity.

Social Pressure

Research studies show that popular teens may face more peer pressure than other teens. They feel they must keep up their looks, wear a certain type of clothing, and act a certain way, or else they may be kicked out of the "in" group.

Some popular teens try to maintain their social position by gossiping and excluding others.

The studies also show that some popular teens have a greater chance of engaging in risky behaviors than other teens. This includes using alcohol or drugs. Part of the reason for this may be if they think that the risky behavior is seen as "cool."[10] There is another hard fact of life about popularity. Someone who is popular one year may not be popular the next. That is why trying to be friends with someone just because he or she is popular is a bad idea.

One popular teen grew tired of the pressures that popularity brought with it. "I was popular and therefore stuck with an isolated image I didn't quite know how to handle. I hid every flaw, every feeling, and every insecurity behind makeup and smiles that weren't real. I didn't understand why I felt so inaccessible. Popularity wasn't supposed to be lonely."[11]

One day at lunch in the school cafeteria, she broke down. She told her friends how "sick she was of all the talk, the walk, the image. I told them that I wanted to be real, that I hurt, that I was confused, just like everybody else." From that time on, she opened herself up to different kinds of people, not just the popular ones. She said this made her much happier with herself and her life.[12]

Another teen found that making a change made her happier, too. When Elizabeth was a sophomore in high school, her best friend told her that they could not be friends anymore. Her friend had a crush on a football player. She thought her friendship with Elizabeth would hurt her chances of getting a date with him because Elizabeth was not part of the "in" crowd.

Later, when Elizabeth was a senior, she talked with the football player her friend had liked and briefly dated. He asked her why the two girls had stopped being friends. When Elizabeth told him what had happened, he said that Elizabeth's friendship would not have made any difference to him.

Elizabeth was glad that she had gone on to find better friends. She said she felt she had greater experiences than she ever would have had with her former friend. Sometimes something may happen that makes you sad, but you may later find, as Elizabeth did, that it leads to a happier life.[13]

Insecurities

Researchers say that many teens worry that no one will like them. They say it identifies the insecurity that young people often feel in their teen years when they are trying to figure out who they are and what they want out of life. There is a strong desire to fit in. For some, this leads to an intense drive to be popular.

"In junior high and high school, I wanted to be popular so badly that I lost myself," says writer Amanda Ford. "Everything I did, the people I talked to, the clothes I wore, and the things I said, were all done to get people to like me."[14]

"Teenagers want to feel that they are part of the 'popular' crowd and sometimes it can get absolutely ridiculous and absurd to what lengths some adolescents will go to just to be accepted," says Howard.[15]

One high school teacher agrees. She says, "Kids resort to behavior that borders on dangerous. . . . They've learned how to manipulate a situation just to be popular."[16]

This desire to be popular can be so strong for some teens that it can stress them out. It can also make them do things they later regret. Amber's best friend, Kerrie, had an overwhelming desire to be popular. Kerrie was thrilled when she was invited to a party given by the most popular boy in school. However, the night ended badly. Kerrie was involved in a car accident when she tried to drive home while she was drunk.

"Kerrie told me she had wanted to fit in so badly at the party that she drank whatever anybody gave her. Everybody was drinking, and she wanted to look as cool as they did," says Amber. Kerrie knew she was in no shape to drive home, but no one would help her. When she tried to drive home herself, she lost control of her car. She hit another car that was stopped at an intersection.

Afterward, Kerrie became involved in the Students Against Drunk Driving (SADD) organization. She now gives talks to high-school teens to warn them about her experience. She hopes by doing this, she might persuade other teens not to do what she did.[17]

As you get older, you may be faced with peer pressure. Some people may try to get you to smoke, take drugs, or drink alcohol. You probably know that these things are harmful. However, sometimes the desire to go along with popular kids can be overwhelming, as Kerrie learned.

Sometimes, a desire to fit in and be accepted causes teens to do things they would normally not do, such as drink or use drugs.

The Truth About Popularity and Appearance

Why do teens place so much value on appearance? Some people think that the media is partly to blame for this. Movies and TV shows feature beautiful people, yet newspaper headlines often reveal that many of these people have troubled personal lives. Teens sometimes focus on the outward appearance of these popular people and ignore the whole picture.

It is normal to want to look good and fit in. It becomes a problem, though, if you spend too much time stressing about it. Instead, work on the things you can change. To a certain extent, you can alter the way you look through diet and exercise. Also, try to remember that your looks will change over time. You won't always look the way you do right now.

"How you look is important. But beauty is a state of mind as well as body. Low self-esteem and constant obsession over food and weight are not healthy, nor do they make you a fun person to be around," says psychologist Marlin Potash.[18]

It can be helpful to realize that popularity—or lack of popularity—is not a lifelong state. Did you know that some of singer Mariah Carey's high school classmates made fun of her outfits? Or that Madonna claims she was unpopular in high school? Pop star Lady Gaga was always teased for her crazy outfits when she was a teenager. Now, her unusual look is part of what makes her famous.

Friendship

You do not have to be popular as a teen to be successful as an adult. In fact, the opposite could be true. Early hardships may help you to learn how to deal with life's challenges. You need to learn to be flexible and to develop coping strategies that will help you to become a happy, successful adult.

"Being constantly dissed by other girls when I was younger made me who I am today—an achiever," says Caitlin.[19]

Accept Yourself

These stories point out something that is extremely important. It is okay to be yourself. The way you look is largely determined by the genes you have inherited from your family. Do not waste your energy into wishing you looked like someone else. Put that energy into working on your own unique qualities.

> Any day of the week
> I would choose to be "out"
> With others
> And in touch
> With myself...
> Than to be "in" with others
> And out of touch
> With myself.[20]

As far as getting into good physical shape goes, there are many choices—running, power walking, swimming, or kickboxing, to name a few. Fitness experts advise people to find some type of exercise or sport they like. If you are having fun, you will not just think of it as exercise. You may even find yourself looking forward to it. Meanwhile, you will be getting into shape.

Getting in shape through exercise can help you feel better about yourself—and it can be fun, too.

Feeling good about yourself should not just be based on what you look like on the outside. It should also come from the kind of person you are like on the inside. There is an old saying that "beauty is just skin deep." This means physical beauty is superficial, and it will fade as time goes by. As you get older, you will realize it is true. Everyone has a desire to belong. But, you should not have to change your own beliefs or risk your personal well-being just to be popular.

Friendship

Author Meg Cabot believes a good personality is more important that good looks when it comes to gaining popularity, despite what many teenagers think. "Planets orbit around the sun. People orbit around sunny people. That's why, if you want to be popular, it's important to radiate warmth and self-confidence. . . . Because, who doesn't love being around a truly happy, cheerful person?"[21]

Chapter 3

Cliques

In some girls' cliques, the members wear similar clothing styles, and choosing the "correct" brands is very important.

Cliques are groups of friends, but not every group of friends is a clique. They are like clubs because they only let certain people join, and they exclude others. Sometimes they do this to make it seem that the teens in their group are "cooler" than other teens. There are also hierarchies of cliques, with the most popular groups sitting pretty at the top of the social ladder, all the way down to the loners.

Not all cliques cause problems. Some are harmless. The important difference is in how members are treated and how members treat teens outside their group. Some cliques expect members to follow certain rules. They may also be expected to only have friends within the group. If teens do not do this, they can be kicked out of the clique. These things make some cliques very limiting because they try to control the way that members behave.

Some cliques have both guys and girls in them, while others are same-sex cliques. Teens may move back and forth in different cliques, trying to find a good match. Overall, membership in a clique is especially important to younger teens.

Female Cliques

"The common definition of a clique is an exclusive group of girls who are close friends. I see it a little differently. I see them as a platoon of soldiers who have banded together to navigate the perils and insecurities of adolescence," says Anastasia Goodstein in her book *Queen Bees and Wannabees.*[1]

Girls have more cliques than guys. These cliques often center on fashion. Emily, Allison, and Anne say they like to dress up a few times a week in dress shirts and fitted pants or skirts. They only wear certain brands of clothes, such as Gap, Old Navy, J. Crew, or Abercrombie & Fitch.

"There's a lot of Abercrombie, especially among the sophomore scene," says Emily. "For the young kids, it's so safe, so acceptable. They cannot be made fun of."

Geeks/Nerds

Although members of this group may have been made fun of in the past, sometimes for lack of social skills, classmates always appreciated them for help with homework. Nerds around the world received a status boost after former high-school nerd Bill Gates shot to fame and became one of the richest men in the world.

The girls joke about what they call the "preemie scene." That is what they call younger teen girls who wear very short skirts along with glitter makeup. Says Allison, "Their hair is made to look like bedhead, but you know it took two hours to do it."[2]

Other commonly found girl cliques might be members of a drill team or dance group. They can often be seen wearing the same uniforms, walking down the school halls together. Because they practice and perform together, they often develop strong bonds, almost a form of sisterhood.

Downsides of Cliques

Cliquey talk and behavior can be a poor influence on young people because it makes fun of others. That can hurt people and make them feel left out. Sometimes teens are left out because they may look or act different or because they do not have cool clothes. Sometimes it is because they have just moved to the area and don't know anyone.

Friendship

"It is devastating to hear people say bad things about you. It hurts your feelings and can ruin your self-esteem," says one teen.[3]

That's not the only downside of cliques. When you are in a clique, you aren't really "allowed" to try to do different things or be with other people who aren't in the clique. In effect, you are letting other people tell you what you can and cannot do. This might result in many missed opportunities.

Why Join a Clique?

Some teens join cliques thinking it might make them more popular. Others join because clique members give each other advice about everything from dating to clothes choices to more serious issues. That gives teens a safety net or lifeline. That can be extremely helpful, especially if teens come from families that do not offer much support.

Amy is part of a group made up of about twenty girls and guys. She says the group watches out for each other. Recently the group decided to tell a boy's parents about his drug problem. The boy later thanked them. She says, "We all rely on each other a lot."[4]

For some students, finding and joining a clique is very important. "Until you have a clique, you're pretty much a loner," says Lauren. After her family moved, she had to enter a new school. She was unhappy for a while, until she found a group that she eventually joined.[5]

Professor Vivian Seltzer says, "Cliques are a part of growing up and being invited in and not being invited in, which is also a part of growing up."[6]

Many times a tween or teen will become upset after someone who has been a good friend starts to pull away and becomes more friendly with another person or a new group. But, Seltzer says, that is normal because adolescence is "a period of great change and growth."[7]

Writer and researcher Rosalind Wiseman says:

> I don't think there's anything wrong per se with cliques. They're natural. Girls tend to have a group of girlfriends with whom they feel close, and often these friendships are great. They share secrets, can be themselves, hang out and act silly, and usually think that they will be supported no matter what. But something in the way girls group together also sows the seeds for the cruel competition for popularity and social status.[8]

Lonely Teens

Teens who are not in a clique can feel as if they are all alone. For example, Derek had friends until he went to a new school. He became unhappy because he did not know anyone there. He said that he "felt alone in the midst of crowds of strangers. I still remember the lonely times of eating lunch by myself, not knowing anyone else and afraid to befriend others."[9]

Friendship

Christine also knows what it is like to feel lonely. She says, "Trying to break into a clique is the hardest thing in the world."[10]

Teens in this situation may feel lonely, angry, and frustrated. Research shows that teens without friends often have low grades as well as low self-esteem. They may also drop out of high school at higher rates than other teens.

Some cliques consist of people involved in the same activity, such as cheerleading, marching band, or theater.

One newspaper article describes this, saying, "Anyone who [has] attended an American high school any time this century knows that teens tend to divide sharply into cliques. These divisions can devastate students who don't easily fit a niche."[11]

Bullies

Something else that can devastate students are the bullies that can sometimes be found in cliques. These teens single out individuals for repeated physical or psychological intimidation. According to the National Association of School Psychologists (NASP), one in seven kids in schools are either a bully or a victim. The NASP says that 160,000 teens stay home from school every day because of bullying.

"Low self-esteem is something both the aggressor and the victim of such attacks share; they just express it differently. Whereas the aggressors gain a sense of power and control, the victims can feel depressed, isolated, and withdrawn," says one counselor.[12]

Not everyone agrees with that idea. In her book *Totally Wired,* writer Anastasia Goodstein says, "Low self-esteem is often a reason given for why kids bully. But, while some girl bullies may have low self-esteem (be insecure and jealous) and mask it with overconfidence, most boy bullies actually have high self esteem and feel exalted."[13] Teasing occurs regularly in high school, even between friends. How do you tell the difference between teasing and bullying? "What distinguishes [a bully] from someone who teases occasionally is a pattern of *repeated* physical or psychological intimidation," writes Allan L. Beane in his book *The Bully Free Classroom*.[14]

Bullying has also changed today because of the Internet. In *Totally Wired*, Goodstein says that bullies today might IM or e-mail threats. "Bullying has expanded to in-boxes, buddy lists, cell phones, and Web pages."[15]

Some ways to deal with teasing:

- Ignore it. Giving teasers any type of response will only encourage them to keep teasing you.

- If they cannot get a reaction from you, they will usually move on.

- If they don't stop, it's time to notify an adult.

The situation gets more serious when teasing turns into bullying—repeated verbal or physical attacks. What you can do about bullying:

- Use humor. If a bully makes fun of your hair or clothes, thank him or her for pointing out that you're having a bad hair day (or a bad clothes day).

- Assert yourself—tell him or her "Stop or I'll report you."

- Confuse the person—keep asking, "What did you say?"

Should you confront a bully? Experts are divided in their opinions about this. Getting into a shouting match could lead to physical violence, and someone could get hurt. If you do confront a bully, don't do it alone. Take a friend or two with you. Also, try to do it when a teacher is nearby, in case help is needed.

One principal says, "We as school people need to become much more tuned into what kids are doing to each other or having done to them. . . . When it comes to unkind behavior and exclusion, kids must learn that you can't do things like that, and that if you do there's a risk."[16]

Leaving a Clique

The teen years are a time when young people are trying to find out where they fit in. Because of that, clique membership can change frequently, with boys and girls moving in and out of different groups, trying to find one that fits them.

If you are in a clique, do not let the group pressure you into doing things you do not want to do. Also, ask yourself whether you are missing out on being friends with other people and activities because of your involvement with the clique. Do you miss old friends, ones who are not in the clique? That is one reason teens say they have left cliques—to get back with old friends.

It could be that before you got into the group, you did not know what the clique was really like. Sometimes cliques purposely give off a certain image just to seem cool. You may have even gone along with what the other members of the clique did, even if you felt it was not really right. It is great that you are aware enough now to see that there is a problem and strong enough to stand up for yourself.

Unfortunately, some cliques harbor bullies. Asserting yourself, using humor, and consulting an adult are three methods of dealing with a bully.

If you have disagreements with the group, you could try talking about your feelings and see what the members say. You may or may not be able to change the opinions of anyone else in the clique, but at least you tried. Be aware, though, that it is often difficult to get other people to change their behavior. They may feel like you are launching a personal attack against them. On the other hand, maybe some other members of the clique secretly feel the same way you do, but they are just too scared to say so. The fact that you are making your thoughts known may inspire them to speak up as well.

Teens who have found themselves in this situation say that it sometimes works best if you gradually withdraw from a clique rather than abruptly leave. That tends to lessen any hurt feelings and may avoid conflict. Others claim it is best to make a quick, clean break. It is up to you to decide what is the best thing for you to do. You know the teens in the group and what they are like.

"A girl who's strong and says 'no' to whatever's bad for her gets to be a leader," says Melody.[17]

When teens Ariana, Christine, and Lauren were in the ninth grade, they wanted to make friends so badly that they joined groups where there was not any real friendship. "You end up with something to cling to, but it doesn't necessarily mean you have real friends," says Ariana.

They eventually left the cliques they were in and formed their own group. They are much happier now, according to Ariana. She says, "This is like a family."[18]

Friendship

Cliques and Stereotypes

Teens have different ideas about cliques and stereotypes. Some think they are bad, while others do not.

"Interact with everyone. People are interesting. If you don't stereotype yourself, you can meet more people. You shouldn't classify yourself, keep yourself open," suggests Stephen.[19]

Andrew says, "Sometimes belonging to the stereotype means you have friends. It benefits you [but can be] used to put other people down."[20]

Stereotypes can be damaging, according to Virgil, because if you're put in a group, you're basically stuck with it.[21]

Although some teens do not mind the labels they have been given by other teens, others don't like them at all. They think that people sometimes don't look past those labels to see what the individual teens are like. For example, Abbie really likes music and has played in the band for four years. "I think that most people consider me a bandie and a nerd. Both are true, but I don't think that's all there is to me," she says.[22]

> **C**linical psychologist Louise Mini asks, "Does your identity come from the outside, so that you need the right car and clothes? If the answer is yes, it may be time to take a less materialistic approach to defining yourself."
>
> Charlene C. Giannetti and Margaret Sagarese, *Cliques* (New York: Broadway Books, 2001), p. 191.

David plays quarterback on his school's football team and is also on the baseball team. He agrees that labels can be misleading: "I guess I am a jock, but I'm not a dumb jock. Most of the people that don't know me would probably consider me a dumb jock. How many jocks [do] you know have a 4.1 GPA for last grading period?"[23]

Outgrowing Cliques

One teen wrote a paper in which he wondered whether he and his friends would mature out of being in cliques when they grew older. "Maybe we'll even remember that golden rule that our moms taught us long ago [to treat others as you would like to be treated]," he said. "And won't the world be a better place?"[24]

Research does show that as teens get older members often outgrow the need to be in a clique. By the time they are high-school seniors, many cliques have thinned out or disappeared. This may be because by this time, teens are more likely to see themselves as individuals rather than as members of a group.

Making Good Choices

The teen years are a time when you should be thinking about your beliefs, values, and interests. Before getting involved with any cliques, ask yourself whether it is a good idea. Do you want to be part of a group because you share its values—or because of a need to feel accepted? Make decisions that match your values and priorities, not someone else's.

Online Friendships and Communication

Teens use the Internet for a number of things—connecting socially, doing homework, playing games, and shopping.

Studies show that what teens do online is very similar to what they do offline. They use the Internet to connect socially, play games, and shop, among other things. They also use it to help with school homework and research projects. Besides these things, many teens like to create their own content, such as Web pages and blogs.[1]

51

"The Internet plays an increasingly important role in kids' friendships. Social networking Web sites aid in youth development by providing an arena to build meaningful relationships, establish independence, strengthen their identity, and become connected to a community that is not limited to their physical community," according to Suzanne Martin, PhD, research manager, Youth and Education Research, Harris Interactive.[2]

Another Internet marketing professional says, "Over half of teens have created some of their own content online: either a blog, a Web page, personal art, or other materials that represent the self. And they're asking their friends to share in it, look at it, be part of it."[3]

Online Friends

One reason why teens like to go online is that it is an easy way for them to connect with others. Many teens believe that you can be friends with anyone, even if you have never met them in person. More than one-third of teens have friends whom they have only "talked" to online.

One benefit of this is that online friends do not base their judgments on how you look, how much money you have, or what kind of clothes you wear. When you have a virtual relationship, the closeness comes from sharing your personal thoughts and feelings instead of your physical presence.

Most teens say they have between one and ten friends. However, that number increases dramatically if they include those on their online profiles on a social networking site or instant messaging (IM) buddy lists. For example, Kendall has several good friends. However, like many other teens, she has found a whole new set of friends online. She has more than two hundred friends on her IM buddy list. Although she has never met them, she thinks these people are an important part of her life.

"I'm talking to kids I never would have talked to before," she says. "I learned that there's so much more to life outside of high school."[4]

Common Online Abbreviations

BRB—Be right back

BTW—By the way

FWIW—For what it's worth

GMTA—Great minds think alike

IMO—In my opinion

IRL—In real life

L8R—Later

TXS—Thanks

Her mother approves of Kendall's Internet use. She says, "They can share stories and get a better understanding of what other teens' lives are like. And they can share issues they may be dealing with with another teen and not have to worry about repercussions in their own social circles."[5] Kate also says that her Internet friends are very important to her. In fact, she thinks her Internet social life is more exciting than her social life offline.

"Online, all you have is words," she says. "In real life, physical characteristics can get in the way. With the Internet, you have time to think about exactly what you want to say. I think you can communicate more honestly than in real life."[6]

She says that at school she sometimes felt isolated from other teens. She preferred listening to music on her headphones instead of talking with her classmates. After school, she would go home and chat with her Internet friends for hours.

"In the physical world, you're only so likely to be able to meet people you click with or share interests," she said. "Online it's like a big phonebook of everyone in the world. . . . I don't know what I would have done if I didn't have online friends."[7]

Online Personalities

Tweens and teens are often struggling to discover who they really are. Many think online communication helps them in that search. Their families and friends know them in a certain way. Online they are free to act differently. Shy teens lose some of their shyness, and the lonely can reach out.

In some cases, teens' online relationships are deeper than their offline relationships. Many teens report that they're more likely to let others see their true selves when they are online. They also say that they share more personal information with friends online than they do face-to-face. They may feel more at ease because they do not actually see the people on the other end of their Internet connection.

Internet Addiction

On average, kids ages twelve to seventeen spend almost eleven hours a week online. One in five younger teens spend twenty or more hours a week online.[8] It's easy to lose track of time when you are on the Internet. When does it all become too much? If someone stops doing other activities he or she has enjoyed over the years, such as sports, music, or hobbies, just to have more time for the Internet, it's probably time to step back and try to get some balance into his or her life.

Writer Julie Taylor says, "Chatting with [online friends] is like writing in a diary with someone on the other end writing back."[9]

Teen Experiences

There are a number of ways to interact online, including instant messaging, blogs, and message boards.

Instant messaging. Elizabeth likes to talk with her friends, often online through instant messaging (IM). The IM software lets anyone with an Internet connection send messages to friends' computer screens. Every day she sits in front of the family's computer for at least an hour. She says, "Most of the time someone's online [whom] I can talk to."[10]

Teens use IM to do some things they used to do face-to-face. One-fifth of teens who use IM have asked out another teen that way. One in seven teens who regularly uses IM has ended a relationship with IM. It's possible that they did it to avoid the face-to-face drama of tears and anger.[11]

Few teens would probably object to being asked out online. However, it is different with breaking up. Then, it may seem too harsh. There are no easy answers as to whether these things should be done this way. If something like this happens to you, the best thing you can do is learn from it and move on.

If you are thinking of breaking up with someone with IM, ask yourself how you'd feel if someone did it to you. You may want to think of a different way to break up, such as in a face-to-face meeting. Before you do anything, give it some thought as to what the best way would be.

Blogging. Jess says that the Internet helped her when she was younger. She used to be extremely shy. "Meeting" people online was easier for her than meeting them face-to-face. That is one of the reasons she started an online journal, or blog (short for Weblog). She writes in it often, sometimes as much as four to five times a day. She says she writes things there that she probably would not say to her friends.

Many teens express themselves by creating their own content on the Internet, through blogs and Web pages.

"I say things that are more poetic that I wish I could say," Jess explains. "Writing's always been more comfortable for me."[12]

She thinks that online communication is a way for teens to feel that they have a voice. When you write something on the Internet, everybody can see it. Also, people who read her blog sometimes leave comments. "For a long time I thought no one would ever care to see it," she says. "Maybe someone will understand it or get some comfort from it."[13]

Many other teens have learned that it is fun to write a blog. There can be all different reasons why they do it. They might want to tell people about a movie they saw, a book they read, or about a new video game that just came out. Others like to use their blogs more like personal diaries or journals. But for all bloggers, it is a way to express themselves creatively and share some aspect of themselves with others. It is a way to connect with other people.

An easy way to learn about blogging is to log onto the Internet and type in "free blogs" in the search box. This will bring up a number of Web sites where you can create a free blog. Choose one of them and then follow the instructions that are found in the section called "create a blog." When you click on it, you will see that anyone can open a blog quickly, usually in three or four steps. Once you do this, you can see how blogging works. Then you can decide whether you want to try it.

There are a number of things to think about if you want to write a blog. Do you enjoy writing? You have to have things you really want to write about. Some people write blogs about high school, music, writing, or taking a long trip. Thousands of others are doing these same things. They can easily relate to them and probably would like to read what you say about them.

Message boards. In addition to blogs, many teens like to use Internet communication groups. These are also called Web forums, discussion boards, or electronic discussion groups. Thousands of message boards exist. Popular board subjects include technology, computers, and video games. However, you can find one on almost any subject. Millions of people read and respond to the messages posted on these message boards.

Message boards are simple to use. You can just go to a Web site and look for a link to a forum on the home page. Or you can type in "message boards" in your browser's search field. Then you can look through the board choices. It may take some time to find one that you like. Or you may find a great one right away. Most boards have some type of search feature. These can help you find messages by topic, date of posting, or name of sender.

Online Social Networking Sites

Some of the most popular Internet sites for teens are social networking sites. These include Facebook and MySpace. As many as half of all online teens use them or similar sites. Social networking sites are places where a user can create a profile and build a personal network. This connects them to other users. Tens of millions of Internet users visit these sites regularly.

Research shows that older teen girls use these sites to talk with their friends. Older boys, however, use them differently. They see the networks as places where they can flirt and make new friends.[14]

MySpace versus Facebook

These two social networking sites were designed for different types of users. In general, MySpace attracts younger teens and features entertainment and music on the site. Facebook was initially designed for older users. Along with using it to connect with friends, it can be used for professional use, as a meeting place for colleagues and business professionals.

Developmental psychologist Jeffrey Arnett describes the way that teens post pictures of themselves online as "a high tech way of expressing an impulse among teenagers and young adults that psychologists call 'the imaginary audience.' This refers to the idea that these young people think others are more interested in them than they actually are."[15]

Because currently reality television shows are very popular, maybe this is a way that teens can take part in the "look at me" experience. Online, they can be stars of a sort.

More than 200 million users have visited MySpace since August 2003. The Web site has been described as a cross between an e-mail program and a diary. Teens also like to use it like a photo album that can be shared with friends.

Teens are always looking for new features and different ways to communicate. During a few months' time, an Internet site can attract tens of millions of users. However, within a few months, millions may decide to leave it and try a second site.

"They're not loyal," says one market analyst. "Young audiences search for innovative and new features. Because of that group mentality, friends shift from service to service in blocs."[16]

". . . [A] lot of my friends have deleted their MySpaces and are more into Facebook now," says Jackie. She has given up on MySpace and spends time now on her Facebook profile, exchanging messages and photos with other teens.[17]

> "Teens who are most active offline, with extracurricular activities such as sports, band, and drama club, tend to be the most active online."
>
> Julie A Evans, "Let's Chat," *Better Homes and Gardens*, September 2007, p. 196.

Her classmate, E. J. Kim, says that she has changed from working over her MySpace profile up to four hours a day to deleting it all together. "I've grown out of it," she says. "I thought it was kind of pointless."[18]

Some teens have decided not to get involved with social networking sites at all. Evan says, "Over time, people are going to get sick of talking to people on the computer. I just think people want to spend more time with each other—without the wall of technology."[19]

Graeme agrees. "I just can't get to grips with the whole MySpace concept. . . . A place you can talk to your friends. I'm sorry, but I can do that outside, in the fresh air, with real people. My social life does not plug into the wall and revolve around a screen on a desk."[20]

Online Games

Another place where teens can make friends online is when they play video games. In MMORPGs (massively multiplayer online role-playing games), such as World of Warcraft and EverQuest, players control an avatar, explore, fight, and complete quests in virtual worlds. Thousands of players sometimes participate in these popular games.

Brandon is a high-school sophomore who plays EverQuest. He thinks the social connections he makes while doing it are important. He says, "An advantage to EverQuest is the social development, an increase in intellect, and exposure to new people and opinions."[21]

A big part of the popularity of games such as EverQuest is that close friendships are formed between the players. While playing MMORPGs, Brandon says, team members do not just kill enemies. They have to strategize. To do that, they have to work together.

One online researcher who conducts online surveys of people who play MMORPGs says, "All of us would like to put our friends into simulated crises to see whether they would stand by us in a time of need. Instead of making friends and then slowly finding out whether they can really be trusted, MMORPG players are making friends with people who have demonstrated that they can be trusted because of their actions."[22]

Speedy Service

One widespread form of online communication is e-mail. It is a great way for teens to stay in touch with friends or to "talk" with other teens they have met online. Some think that e-mail

Networking Numbers

The top five things teens post online:

First name—82%

Personal photo—79%

City or town—61%

School name—49%

IM screen name—40%

What teens think about online practices:

81% think it is okay to tell someone they just met online where they live.

71% think it is okay to tell online friends where they go to school.

29% would give out their cell phone numbers to online friends.

19% would give out their home phone numbers to online friends.[23]

New technologies have made it easier than ever to stay in touch. But the "instant" nature of such communication can sometimes cause problems—so think before hitting "send."

has become the number-one method of communication in the modern world. It has a lot going for it because e-mailing is fast, easy, and inexpensive.

"I haven't met Geneva in person, but she's one of my closest friends. I feel like she knows the real me. We e-mail and instant message each other at least five times a day. Even though she lives across the country, she's always close to my heart," says Sara.[24]

However, e-mail has one drawback. Users have found out too late that once you hit the "send" button, your e-mail is gone. Whatever words you may have used are also out there forever. You cannot take them back.

In many cases, that is okay. That is what you wanted. But have you ever gotten angry at someone and written an e-mail saying things you felt at the time, then later realized you may have overreacted or completely misunderstood what had happened? Then, you may have wished you could take your e-mail back.

Friendships have been strained and even ended because of e-mails. Because of this, take a minute to think before you send an angry-sounding e-mail. It could help you avoid some embarrassment and maybe even save a friendship.

Be sure to observe Internet safety guidelines when you are communicating with your online friends. Teens have experienced incidents ranging from false identity to kidnapping to death through their Internet connections. Have fun, but stay safe.

Don't post any personal information online, such as your telephone number, last name, address, school, or anything that would allow a stranger to know how to contact you face-to-face. Also, many teens use screen names that do not reveal whether they are male or female.

Chapter 5

Making Friends

"**Whenever I meet someone new, I just freeze up.** I never know what to say or how to start a conversation with them. I end up feeling like such a loser," says one teen.[1]

It takes some courage to engage in a conversation with a complete stranger, whether you approached him or he approached you. It takes a little bit of trust to open up, and trust isn't something that automatically appears out of thin air.

66

Friendship

Another teen confesses, "Every time I meet someone new, I feel like I'm holding back so much. I only let them know like 50 percent of who I am. I don't know. I guess I have a hard time trusting people and don't know how to let my guard down sometimes."[2]

Easy or Hard?

When you are young, it's usually easy to make friends. You just walk up to someone who looks friendly and start talking. Most small children do not feel self-conscious or awkward about meeting new people. Things change, though, when children become teens. A lot more thought goes into the process. Sometimes insecurities can overcome them, and they hesitate before talking to someone new. They worry that the person won't like them for some reason.

Although some make friends easily, for most people making friends is a skill. Just like practicing on the piano, your ability to make friends will improve the more you work at it.

Your Secret "Weapon"

Whether you know it or not, you possess one thing that can help you make friends. You can use it in situations that can be unnerving, such as your first day at a new school, having to get up in front of a class and give a speech, or trying to find a place to sit in a crowded cafeteria. Your secret "weapon" is your smile. It can be a powerful communication tool.

Even if smiling is the last thing you feel like doing, do it. It can achieve powerful results. Studies have shown that a smile can boost your mood—even when your smile is a fake.

Linda says:

> There's a girl at my school who always smiles. Even if she doesn't know you that well, she'll say "hi" in the halls, and she always has funny stories to tell. You feel special that she took the time to notice you and talk to you even though . . . you might not be one of the people closest to her. She inspires me to do the same—to go out and smile and be friendly to others that I don't know so well, either.[3]

Making new friends gets easier with practice. Greeting someone with a smile is a good way to start.

Friendship

Another teen says:

My freshman year of high school, I decided to audition for a play. When I showed up at auditions, I didn't know anyone in the room and was sitting by myself studying the script, trying not to be nervous. Suddenly this girl sitting like five feet away from me gave me this huge smile. My first reaction was, "Wow, she's really nice," before she even came over and introduced herself. And guess what, we've been friends ever since.[4]

Look Around

As these two teens learned, school is a good place to find friends. Look around in your classes. You probably already have some things in common with other students there. Is there someone whom you say "hi" to every day? It's possible that this person has already become a friend. You just may not have thought about him or her that way.

Another way to meet people is to join a school club or a sports team. These can be good places to meet potential friends because you'll probably have similar interests with others there.

Outside school, go to places that you enjoy, and find teens there with interests that are similar to yours. This could be a sports event, a church function, a dance, or something else. Some teens also say they have made some good friends at after-school jobs.

Possible conversation starters:

- "What was the assignment?"

- "Can I sit here?

- "You're really good at that."

- "Did you study for the quiz?"

- "How long have you been interested in (fill in a subject)?"

Communication Skills

You can improve your communication skills the same way that you improve at spelling, sports, or video games. Some people may have more natural talent at this than others. Everyone else has to work at them. Successful athletes, musicians, carpenters, mechanics, and business executives all became experts by practicing their skills over and over.

Here are a few tips that can help you when you are talking with others:

- Look at the person you are talking to—looking at a person shows that you are interested and paying attention.

- Be relaxed (or at least look relaxed)—avoid behaviors that show you are nervous or tense, such as looking away, looking down at the floor, staring at your hands, or fidgeting.

Friendship

Quiz: Making Friends 101

1. Name three places at school where you might make friends.
2. What are some things you could say to start up conversations?
3. What could you do to bring a new friend and old friends together?
4. Name three things you can do to help you deal with shyness.
5. Name three places away from school where you could make friends.

• Don't interrupt or monopolize the conversation.

• Ask questions—people usually feel good when others show an interest in them.

Use your voice to your advantage—you send signals with your voice. That means you can sound interested, concerned, sympathetic, upset, silly, etc.

Once you have exchanged a few sentences, keep talking. Ask follow-up questions. Express interest in what the other person has to say. Most people like to talk about themselves.

By watching the person's body language and facial expressions, you should be able to tell whether the person is interested in talking to you or not. If not, don't stress. It may just be a matter of bad timing. Try another time. She could have just had a fight with her mom or just be having a bad day.

Find someone else and start talking. The world is a big place. There are sure to be people out there who would be good friends. You just have to find them.

Make a Move

"When I changed schools . . . I knew no one, and I mean not a single soul. I would go straight from school to my room and cry the rest of the day, feeling sorry for myself," said one teen.[5]

Then, one day a girl in her English class asked her if she knew where the basketball team tryouts were. It turned out that she was new, too. She said she had decided to try to join clubs as a way of meeting people. The two girls quickly became friends.

If you want to make some new friends, you can't just sit there and wait for them to come to you. You could be waiting a long time if you did that. You have to make an effort to go out and meet people. It is often just a matter of taking the first step.

Or, you could get lucky, and a friendly person might reach out to you. At that point, you have to grab the opportunity. For example, Marco was a lonely teen who wanted some friends, but he wasn't sure where or how to find them. One day, he met a friendly person who reached out to him. "She saw me sitting alone behind the school one day and invited me to lunch with her and her friends. I accepted, and we have been best friends ever since."[6]

One way to meet people is to join a club, sports team, or volunteer group.

Ways to Find Friends

Teen expert Donna Dale Carnegie suggests three possible "experiments" to try to find some new friends:

1. For the next week, try to smile as often and at as may people as possible. Try to look natural when you do it. You don't want to look fake—you want to look friendly. At the end of the week, ask yourself how people reacted. How did your "experiment" make you feel?

2. Take part in an activity outside school, even if it's only a one-day event. It could be volunteering at a city-wide clean up, working at an animal shelter, taking a class, or something else. Afterward, ask yourself how it felt to be in a new environment. Was it fun? Did you meet anyone new?

3. Choose a person whom you would like to know better. Try opening up to this person, as you would to a friend. How did the person react? How did you feel afterward?

Overall, how did the three experiments work for you? Did you make any new friends? Do you think these things were worthwhile, maybe even fun?[7]

New Students

Another possible way to make some new friends is to talk to teens who have just moved to your area. If you have ever been lonely, or had to eat lunch in the cafeteria by yourself, you might want to help out another teen who is in that same situation. Teens who have just moved and who are new to your school are looking for friends. They could also probably use a little help.

Make an effort and look around you to see if there is anyone who looks like he or she could use a friend. Why not go up and introduce yourself? Ask the person how he or she likes the school. This will be a good way to meet people, and you will be helping someone else, too.

Psychologist Marlin Potash says that it usually takes about six months to adjust after a move. She suggests "flipping your thinking and riding it out." "Yes, it's hard to start over, but it can also be fun," she says. "You're entering a time in life when you might want to bury some of the things from your past and start new."[8]

New Friends/Old Friends

After meeting some new friends, you'll probably want to introduce them to your old friends. Be careful when you do this. Sometimes old friends may feel jealous or threatened when that happens. They may think you might not want to be friends with them anymore now that you have some new friends. Or your new friends may feel awkward around others who have shared so many experiences with you.

Why not do something all together? When you do, be sure to introduce everyone to each other. Try to spend time mixing with everyone. Talk with each person so no one feels left out. That will help ease any awkwardness they might feel and help people relax and have fun.

If the situation were reversed, how would you feel if one of your good friends made a new friend? Sometimes it's hard not to feel jealous and to wonder how this new friendship will affect you. Try to be positive and get to know the person. You may gain another friend that way.

Friendship Rules

Just as with many other things in life, there are some rules for friendship. Start a new friendship off right by following them:

- Do things together.
  Be honest.
- Share ideas, hopes, fears, and dreams.
- Encourage one another to do what's right.
  Be trustworthy and trusting.
- Talk over problems and disagreements.
- Listen to each other.[9]

Finding Your Own Way

There are all different ways to interact with people. All persons are unique and have their own ways to express themselves and to connect with other people. Find a way that you are comfortable with. For example, do you have a particular talent you would like to share with others? Below are a few examples of how young people found a way to connect with people.

"Music is a powerful force in my life," says Brooke Allison, teen vocal artist featured in Disney's *Cinderella II: Dreams Come True*. "I've been singing since I was three. I was very shy when I was a child, but if you put me on stage to perform, all of a sudden I became free."[10]

She says, "You can express your feelings through music. When you listen to my songs, you know exactly what I am going through because I put it into music. When I get stressed out, writing and listening to music helps me relax."[11]

What are your interests and hobbies? Are there any teams or groups you can join in these areas? Making the first step and reaching out will be the hardest part—but once you have made it, you will start to blend in.

It takes a lot of courage to get over the anxiety of approaching people to make friends.

To meet people, one teen says, "I joined the tennis team. I'm not that good, but I love playing. So I figured I might find a partner to play with."[12]

Shyness

For some people, one obstacle to making friends is shyness. If you are shy, it can be hard to make the first move in a friendship or to even respond when someone wants to be your friend.

Shyness is basically a fear of people. That's why shy people feel uncomfortable in social situations.

Research has shown that if you don't do something about this, shyness will continue to control you and your life. There are some steps you can take to make things better for yourself. Your shyness will not disappear overnight, but you will see some positive differences. One technique is to consciously act the way you want to feel, just like an actor playing a role in a movie or TV show. People who have tried this say the "fake it till you make it" method works. The idea behind this is that it takes some of the anxiety away from the situation because you are thinking about your actions rather than about your anxieties.

> "You can make more friends in two months by becoming genuinely interested in people than you can in two years by trying to get people interested in you."
>
> Donna Dale Carnegie
> *How to Win Friends and Influence People for Teen Girls*
> (New York: A Fireside Book, 2005), p. 65.

It may take some time and effort before you can ease your shyness. Like many other things in life, you will get better at it with practice. Think of it as time well spent.

If your shyness has gotten to the point that it prevents you from doing things you would like to do, it may be time to talk to an adult about it.

Party Fears

If you get the jitters before going to a social event, such as a party, you might want to try using a relaxation technique that has worked for others. Close your eyes and visualize yourself at the party, acting relaxed and confident, having fun. Try to make it feel so real that you can actually see yourself talking to people. Use all your senses, imagining how it will sound, look, etc. Try to think what people might say to you and how you might reply.

Go to the party with a friend, which should help you feel relaxed. Once there, feel yourself going through the same events you went through mentally before the party. The idea behind this is that you have already done it once—in your imagination. Since you've already prepared yourself, it could lessen your anxiety.

When you're at the party, remember to take a few deep breaths and smile. People are more apt to come over and talk to you if you look confident and relaxed. Start a conversation with just one person at a time, which may be easier than joining a group. With practice, each time you do this, the next dance, party, or other social event will be a little easier. Transforming yourself from a wallflower to a social butterfly is not the easiest thing in the world. It will take time and effort, but the results will be worth it.

Having a common goal or project—such as a political campaign—can make socializing easier.

Another visualization technique is to think of a place where you feel totally relaxed—maybe at the beach, or in a forest, or somewhere else. Any time you feel stressed, picture that place in your mind and mentally go there. People who do this say it has an immediate calming effect. Tips for visualization:

○ Try to get into a completely relaxed state.

● Use all five senses.

● Practice, practice, practice.

"Don't try too hard. Don't sit there stressing about what to say to make people like you. Trust me, the more you try to be funny and 'cool,' the less you'll be successful," says Lili.[13]

Friends Can Change Your Life

People have different needs when it comes to friends. Some are happy with just a few close friends. Others like having lots of friends. Only you can decide what's the right number for you.

If you want to meet new people, you won't meet them by just sitting in your room and thinking about it. You have to go out and do something about it. Although it may not always be easy, it is important to make friends. Besides the fact that friendships can be fun, they can keep you moving in the right direction.

Teen Guys and Girls

Learning about the differences in how boys and girls communicate can make it easier to talk with members of the opposite sex.

Thirteen-year-old Irene says, "I'm fine when it comes to talking with my girlfriends, but whenever I'm around guys I get so nervous, it's like, I don't know what's going on in their heads, and I don't have a clue what they want to hear."[1]

Have you ever thought that there was something different about the ways that guys and girls talked and the ways they listened? If so, you are right. Studies have shown that males and females really do have different ways of communicating. Learning about these differences can help you improve your communication skills. They may even help your friendships. You might find some of them surprising. Some things you thought were straightforward may not be that way at all.

What Girls Do for Fun

If you ask a group of girls what they do for fun, they will tell you that they sometimes do silly things. For example, actress Mandy Moore reveals that, "Two of my friends and I had this huge pig-out with chocolate-chip cookie dough, s'mores, popcorn, Doritos. What else? Candy galore."[2]

The fun actually has a purpose, though. While they did that, they probably talked and laughed. Whatever girls do, while they are at the beach, shopping at the mall, or at a football game, the girls are talking and exchanging information. They are getting caught up with what is going on in everyone's lives. Girls love to talk about what they are thinking and feeling. Their conversations bond them together.

"Having close friends gives girls self-esteem, offers much-needed support, and provides unforgettable memories," says teen expert Carol Weston.[3]

Girls Can Be Serious

Of course, girls are not always silly. Sometimes something happens that rattles them, maybe even scares them. Maybe one has heard her parents talking about getting a divorce, or has

What can look like silly behavior actually has a purpose: it binds the members of a group closer together and allows them to share information.

Friendship

had her parents announce that her family has to move. If she has true friends, they will rush to offer her comfort and advice. They will try to soothe their friend's fears and promise to stick close by her through whatever it is that she is going through. There may be tears, but some of them will be tears of gratitude to have such great friends.

Guys React Differently

Teen guys are very different from girls in that most do not like to talk about their feelings. If something bad happens to a guy, he will not hurry to tell his friends about it. He is more likely to get quiet. But his friends can tell that something is wrong. However, they probably won't ask him about it. They say it's a guy thing, and that he probably just wants to be left alone.

That is because guys generally do not like to show their emotions. Most would do anything to avoid having anyone see them cry. They would be afraid of having someone make fun of them and spreading it around. Instead, they would tell themselves to "suck it up."

"Some boys have a macho image that they feel they have to live up to, including never revealing their emotions and acting like they are in control all the time," says psychologist Marlin Potash.[4]

They bond with other males by doing things together. They like to hang out with their friends, seeing which one can think up the funniest or grossest comeback. They will go to an all-you-can-eat pizza place and have a contest, eating until they are almost sick. They will play sports—any kind, anywhere. They are crazy about winning, and many are very competitive— seeing who can get the most home runs, most touchdowns, etc.

Why They Are Different

Some experts believe there are physiological reasons why males and females deal with their emotions differently. Females may be able to better use both sides of their brains, increasing their skill at verbal and emotional expression.

Also, hormones determine how females and males handle their feelings. For females, their estrogen/progesterone causes them to cycle up and down with their moods. In contrast, the male testosterone hormone drives guys more aggressively. They are focused on efficient and quick solutions.[5]

Our culture also plays a part in the way that people think guys and girls react with their emotions. Traditionally, girls are believed to be more emotional and more likely to cry. Guys are expected to be tough—too tough to cry, for example. Many people still believe these stereotypes.

Another important factor when talking about teens is that girls mature more quickly than guys. Males will catch up to girls developmentally by the time they are high-school seniors. That will bring big changes in how they act and talk. However, there will still be basic differences in the ways that guys and girls communicate.

Friendship

Guys often bond by doing competitive things, such as shooting hoops.

Ask your friends, parents, grandparents, or other people about the differences in the ways that males and females communicate. It may even differ by culture or by generation in addition to gender. You may get some surprising answers. Some of them may be funny. However, sometimes these differences can cause misunderstandings and arguments.

Waiting for a Phone Call

Guys and girls use the phone differently to communicate. Girls tend to call each other often. Some can talk for hours about anything and everything. That is why they may become frustrated when they are hoping or expecting guys will call them. They usually wait . . . and wait and wait. The calls may never come, at least not as soon as they expect it.

There can be several reasons for this. Some young male teens may feel hesitant or awkward about calling girls. Also, males in general don't like the long phone calls so common for some females.

An easy solution would be just for a girl to call the guy rather than to wait for him to call her. Some girls do not want to do that. Others think it is okay. You have to decide for yourself what would be best for you to do.

Today, a girl might simply text a guy, saying "hi." This friendly gesture might result in his replying. At least she knows she made an effort to find out how he feels.

Just Friends?

Once, guys and girls did not often have the friends-only relationships with each other that many teens have today. Girls were mostly friends with other girls, and males usually had other guys as friends. Over the years that has changed. Today, many teens have friends of the opposite sex.

Quiz: Guys and Girls

1. You just got a new boyfriend/girlfriend. One of your other friends is worried you won't have time for him/her anymore. What do you do?
   - a) Laugh—of course that's true.
   - b) Tell him/her that's not true, even though you know it will probably happen.
   - c) Assure your friend you will make time for him/her.

2. Your best friend just announced he/she has a new girlfriend/boyfriend. What do you do?
   - a) Warn her/him that it won't last.
   - b) You tell him/her you're happy for them, but you secretly hope they break up.
   - c) You're happy for him/her.

3. You really don't like the girl/guy your friend is dating. The person isn't abusive or anything. You just think your friend could do better. What do you do?
   - a) Lie and tell your friend their boyfriend/girlfriend is cheating on them in hopes of breaking them up.
   - b) Talk to the person to try to find out things you can tell your friend that will hurt their romance.
   - c) Give the person a chance.

Mostly As—A good friend wouldn't say or do these things.

Mostly Bs—Still not very nice.

Mostly Cs—Good choices.

These types of relationships have many benefits. They can help young people learn about the other sex without all the problems of dating. They also tend to be low-key and relaxed. That is welcomed in the tween or teen years, which can often be filled with various social anxieties.

Some people do not believe these friends-only relationships can exist. Television programs and movies often show these relationships changing to romantic ones. That deepens the overall impression that a friends-only relationship usually leads to romance.

What Teens Say

"I don't know why it is so hard for people to believe that males and females can be best friends. I like the male-female relationship because it's less dramatic. Guys don't seem to be as sensitive about things as girls can sometimes be," says Destiny.[6]

Mandy, age sixteen, agrees: "I've been great friends with Trevor since seventh grade. He helps me with my crushes, and I help him with his. Plus, he never acts catty like some of my girlfriends do. He's always mellow and low-key, no matter what's going on around him. He's truly the best guy I know."[7]

Another teen, David, describes his relationship with a girl. "I totally love Renee, but not in a romantic way. I feel totally comfortable around her, I mean, she sees my silly side and that's rare. But romantic? No way. We just don't have that . . . sizzle."[8]

Friendship

Bill says his best friend is a girl named Marlene. He says that when he is with her and his other female friends, he feels free to show his sensitive side. With his guy friends, he always feels the pressure to be macho and talk "guy stuff." Bill loves what he calls "girl energy." He says, "With my friends who are girls, I don't have to put on airs. I can just be me."[9]

Bill's relationship with Marlene allows him to learn about the opposite sex in a nonthreatening environment. She also gives him hints about his romantic relationships from a female's perspective. This is a positive relationship for him, one that helps him grow.

Today, many teens have friends of the opposite sex. Such relationships don't necessarily develop into romantic ones.

What Others Think

If you do have a good friend of the opposite sex, even though you both know that you are just friends, this does not mean that everyone will believe that. Others may assume that you are going out with that person. Sometimes this can cause problems for one or both of you.

For example, Malancha had a good friend who was a guy. They had a lot of fun together and enjoyed their friendship. However, the situation became complicated. Malancha's guy friend had a girlfriend who felt threatened by her. Also, some of their classmates assumed that Malancha and her guy friend were going out. Someone started rumors about them, and before long, the rumors were all over school. That made the situation extremely stressful.

> "If you find someone that you can talk to, that you can trust, and have fun with, why not be a friend with that person, regardless of what sex they are?"
>
> Nancy Krulik
> *The Friendship Hotline: Friends: How to Make 'Em, How to Keep 'Em* (New York: Price Stern Sloan, 1999), p. 40.

Neither Malancha nor her friend knew how to handle the situation, so their friendship died. Afterward, Malancha said, "I wish I was more honest with him in the beginning. I wish I hadn't let his girlfriend, our friends, our families, or our classmates get in the way, because I lost a pretty good friend."[10]

Preventing Clashes

Suggestions for dealing with friends/relationships:
- Don't get involved with the ex of a friend.
  Don't try to steal a boyfriend or girlfriend away from a friend.
- If you do have a girlfriend/boyfriend, try not to talk about him/her all the time.

If you ever find yourself in this type of situation, try to be sensitive to the feelings of all those involved. Your friend's girlfriend or boyfriend may feel jealous and unsure that you are really just a friend. Get to know the person. Try to show him or her that you are not a threat to them or their relationship.

Communication Problems

If you learn to communicate better, you may be able to avoid some of the problems that Malancha faced. When people communicate, they do so verbally, with words, and also nonverbally, through body language and facial expressions. Because of this, even though you tell people one thing, your facial expressions and body language may give them the impression you actually mean something else.

Research has shown that at least 55 percent of communication is physiological—how you sit, move, and look. Thirty-eight percent is tonal (the tone of your voice), and only 7 percent is actually the words you use. Surprisingly, that means that roughly 93 percent of everything you communicate has nothing to do with what you say. If you make sure that your body language and facial expressions match what you are saying, your communication ability will skyrocket.[11]

Writer Bill Beausay tested this by making statements to a group of teens and then contradicting his statements with his actions. For example, he told them, "Bill Clinton is a great president," while shaking his head from side to side. Next, he said, "Let's get this room cleaned up," as he walked around, throwing things on the floor. At first the teens were confused, but in the end they decided they believed his actions, rather than his words.[12]

Because of this, when you're talking to your friends, be aware that they are getting other signals from you besides what you are saying. They're also watching your body language and facial expressions and listening to the tone of your voice, and forming their opinions from this.

What If a Friends-Only Relationship Changes?

What do you do if you realize that your feelings have changed, and that your friendship with someone of the opposite sex is developing into something more? One teen says, "I think it's really hard to be close without . . . feeling like you want to be more than just friends with that person."[13]

Friendship

Dating 411

Things to consider when going on a date:

- Are you going alone with your date, double-dating, or in a group?

 Where are you going?

- What time will you be home?
- Who is driving?

Think carefully before you act. You risk losing the friendship if the relationship does not work out. You could ask, "Have you ever thought about us being more than just friends?" That way, you will know how the other person feels before you go any further. No one else needs to get involved. This could save you from any embarrassment or awkwardness that might happen if your friend feels differently than you do.

Dating

The next step in relationships is dating. Some teens start to date early, while others wait until later. That is okay. Everyone is different. Many early "dates" may be nothing more than you and your friend going somewhere in a group. For young teens, this may be more relaxing and fun than going on a date as a couple. Another benefit is that if you are in a group, you can see how the other teens act with their dates.

Today, not all dating relationships are boy-girl. Gay couples face all the challenges that boy-girl couples face, and more. They may also have problems with their parents and/or friends over the relationship.

Experts say that the chances that a teen relationship will succeed increase if the pair does not rush the relationship, and if they become friends first. If they have developed communication skills, they have a better chance of surviving hard times. It also gives them time to find out what they have in common.

Experts say that a teen relationship has better chances of success if the guy and girl are friends first and do not rush things.

Friendship

A Friend in Need

If one of your friends has a romantic breakup:

• Be there for him or her.
  Be willing to listen to the story over and over again.

• Don't say, "I told you so."

Young teens may sometimes think they are in love. It can be confusing because they have never experienced this before. They may mistake infatuation for love.

With infatuation:

• You are intensely attracted to a particular characteristic that someone has—his or her eyes, smile, or body.

• You feel yourself being swept away by this person whenever you are with him or her.

• You are so attracted to this person that you do not pay attention to the whole person. You overlook their faults.

Infatuation:

• Can be emotionally exhausting.

• Can make you act irresponsibly.

• Can make you feel jealous or possessive.

• Usually disappears as quickly as it appeared.[14]

In contrast, real love is based on friendship, trust, and concern for the other person. You look at the whole person instead of just one feature. Also, instead of happening quickly, it usually develops over time.

Friends Can Be Affected

Whether you are a girl or a guy, when you enter into a romantic relationship, it can affect your friendships. Your friends may feel left out. You are not as available to them as much anymore. You are probably spending time that you used to spend with them with your new girlfriend or boyfriend.

That is why, even if you are in a new relationship, it is important to keep in touch with your friends. Schedule time when you can catch up with what is going on in each other's lives. Let your friends know that they are still important to you. Many teen relationships do not last very long. After they end, your friends will still be there waiting for you.

One teen says, "Don't let a girlfriend or boyfriend get in the way of a friendship. Friends aren't a part-time job; you can't just take six months off because you get in a relationship and then pop back in when you're on your own again."[15]

Attitude

Teen years are full of changes and challenges. Staying true to yourself can take courage.

The teen years are filled with changes.

You are developing physically and mentally and are facing many new social situations. You probably also have many unanswered questions: What kind of life do you want? How can you get it? One thing that will have a strong impact on your future success is your attitude.

Your attitude affects everything you do. It determines the way you see life and the choices you make. The way you look at challenges affects their outcome. Optimism, good will, and self-reliance have helped many people navigate through life's challenges successfully, and they can help you, too.

Making Good Choices

During your tween and teen years, some of your friends may do things that make you feel uncomfortable. At first, you may go along with them to avoid trouble. However, eventually you will have to make a decision about what is going on.

Fifteen-year-old Ellen says:

> There is one girl who I go skiing with a lot in the winter. . . . I guess you could say she's one of the cool people. But she's into doing a lot of stuff that I'm not comfortable with. She started asking me to come with her and do things I knew were not good for me—like making out randomly with guys. I just kind of stopped hanging out with her because I didn't want to deal with the pressure of having to say no.[1]

Ellen's decision to free herself from this relationship took courage. Having to say "no" can be uncomfortable. Don't let yourself be influenced by the actions of others if they go against your personal beliefs. Learn to make smart decisions and then have the courage to stand up for yourself.

You have to live with the choices you make. Even if your parents or other friends never find out what you did, you will know. Some of the choices you make now will affect you for the rest of your life. That's why it is important that you make good ones.

A Determined Attitude Helps

Anna Liu also found out that she had to dig deep within herself to find the best way to handle a difficult situation. At first when she learned she would have to get glasses, she didn't think it was a problem. She picked out a pair that she thought looked good on her. Everything was fine until she went to school the next day.

Some of her friends and classmates started to make fun of the way she looked. She tried to ignore them, but others kept teasing her. Finally, she started to cry. Even then, they didn't let up. One girl told her to stop crying because she looked so messy. By that time, Anna was angry, embarrassed, and frustrated. She pulled off her new glasses and broke them.

Later, after she had calmed down, she thought about what had happened. She knew it was wrong for the other kids to have acted the way they did. But she had allowed herself to become so stressed that she lost control and broke her own glasses. As she went with her mother to get another pair of glasses, she promised herself that she would not lose her self-control again. She wouldn't give the teasers any satisfaction.

The next day, when she wore her glasses to school, the teens started to tease her again. This time she forced herself not to react. The teens stopped their teasing when they saw they weren't going to get any tears from her.

> "People are just about as happy as they make up their minds to be."
>
> Abraham Lincoln.

She later wrote about what had happened to her for her school paper. Afterward, several girls came up to her and told her that her article helped them know one thing to try if they were teased. Anna Liu felt good about that, saying, "Now they knew they were not alone."[2]

Some things you should remember about teasing:

- Realize that teens who do this are often insecure.

- Teasing may be a way of trying to be friendly; it depends on the extent and the tone.

- Some say that showing any response to them will only encourage the teasers.

- Some suggest using humor to deflect teasing.

- If it continues or turns mean, tell a teacher or another adult.

You Can Do It

Have you ever heard of someone who has a "can-do" attitude? When that person is faced with a problem, he or she tries to see it as a challenge. Thinking about something that way removes some of the anxiety from the situation. That frees you to come up with solutions and options to solve a problem rather than simply panicking.

When you are a teen, it may seem nearly impossible to imagine what's in store for you in life. What do you think would help you the most? Thinking about all the possible bad things that could happen to you? Or accepting the fact that life won't be easy, but that you will work hard and do your best?

Can-do people:

- Work to make the things they want happen.

- Think about solutions and actions.

- Act.

Changing Your Mind

Just as Anna Liu had to change her thinking, you may also have to do this sometimes. For example, have you ever thought you knew what was going on in a situation and later found out that you were wrong?

"As a junior in high school, I had a friend named Kim," Becky said. "She was essentially a nice person, but as the year progressed, it became more and more difficult to get along with her. She was easily offended and often felt left out. She was moody and difficult to be around. It got to the point where my friends and I started calling her less and less. Eventually we stopped inviting her to do things." Becky later learned that Kim's parents were going through a messy divorce. She felt terrible that she had deserted her friend without really trying to find out what was going on with her. "Just by knowing that one little bit of information, my whole attitude toward her changed. It was really an eye-opening experience."[3]

Sometimes experiences like this can be painful, but you can learn from them and handle things differently in the future. It is likely that if anything like this happens again, Becky will talk with her friend. She will try to find out what's happening rather than just give up on him or her. You may be unaware of some problems that your friend is facing.

Monica also had an eye-opening experience that changed her attitude: "I used to live in California, where I had a lot of good friends. I didn't care about anybody new because I already had my friends. I thought that new people should deal with it in their own way. Then, when I moved, I was the new kid and wished that someone would care about me and make me part of their group of friends. I see things in a very different way now. I know what it feels like to not have any friends."[4]

Friendship

Monica learned how hard it can be to move to a new school where you don't know anyone. You may go from having many friends to not knowing anyone, as she did. Sometimes you have to experience things for yourself before you understand how different situations can make other people feel. It's likely that Monica treated new kids very differently after her experience.

Keeping Track

Why not start a journal so you can write about all the things that are going on in your life? Keeping a journal can help make you aware of feelings you didn't even know you had. So, next time something happens, you can get your notebook out and write about it.

One of the things people like about keeping journals is that when you read back through some of your journal entries, you can sometimes see patterns or trends in the way you respond to things. This might help you make better decisions. It can help you distance yourself emotionally, too.

Some people use journals to identify stresses and how they made them feel (both physically and emotionally). What was your reaction—being in a rotten mood, pigging-out, getting a headache, etc.? Now that you're aware of the problem, next time you get stressed, maybe you can find a better way to deal with it.

Each friendship is different. Some end when people's interests and activities change; others may last a lifetime.

Accepting Changes

Because friendships are so important, it's sometimes hard to imagine them ending. As you get older, though, you may find that friends whom you were close to when you were younger may not seem right for you anymore. People's interests change as they get older. It's a natural part of growing up. These changes can challenge many friendships.

As these differences surface, most teens try to make adjustments. They may try some of the new things their friends now like, such as listening to a different kind of music, trying a new sport, or meeting some different kinds of people. Sometimes this works, and sometimes it doesn't. In the end, although it may be painful, it is best not to force a friendship if it doesn't work anymore.

Each friendship is different. Some maybe were only meant to last a short while. A few, if you are lucky, may last for years.

If a friendship breaks up and you really don't understand it, you may want to:

- Consider writing a letter, asking why it happened, and expressing your feelings.

- Talk to another friend or adult about it.

- Focus on making new friends.

Colin says:

I've grown apart from friends who lived right next door and stayed close with friends who moved all the way across the country. While some friends will go and new friends will come, the worst possible thing we can do is to grow apart from our own needs. Growing apart from friends, although painful, can often make room for new friends and new experiences.[5]

"When one door closes, another opens. But we often look so regretfully on the closed door that we don't see the one that has opened for us," said Alexander Graham Bell.[6]

The Importance of Listening

One thing that can help you keep your friends and make them feel appreciated is to listen to them when they want to talk. Many people don't really listen to what others say. This can hurt feelings and maybe even end friendships.

"I have a friend who is sometimes good to talk to, but she gets easily distracted. You'll be talking to her, and all of a sudden she'll start talking about something else. Or, she'll be watching TV, and all of a sudden she'll start laughing and I'll realize she's just not listening to me," says fourteen-year-old Jennifer.[7]

If you show a genuine interest in other people and in what they are saying, the results will be worth your time and attention. Teens especially appreciate people who really listen to them. If they don't, it can make teens feel that the person doesn't care that much about them or their problems.

Writer Ericka Lutz says, "Listening is an art. A lot of times people hear what they want to hear, not what's really being said."[8]

You usually can tell if someone is really listening and paying attention to what you're saying. They probably aren't truly listening if they interrupt you, rush to give their own opinions, or don't respond to what you have said.

Quiz: A+ Attitude

1. One of your friends has just told you that his parents are getting a divorce. He's really upset. What should you do?

>   a) You don't know what to say—so you start avoiding him.
>   b) You tell him that lots of parents divorce.
>   c) You make a point of listening to him whenever he wants to talk.

2. A friend starts getting emotional about graduation. You:

>   a) Avoid the person.
>   b) You don't know what to say, so you make jokes about it.
>   c) Tell him that the two of you can keep up your friendship through calls and e-mails.

3. You've just heard that one of your friends gossiped about you behind your back. You:

>   a) Drop the person as a friend.
>   b) Give her a dirty look every time you see her.
>   c) Go to the person and ask if she really said it.

>   **Mostly As**—You can do better than this.
>   **Mostly Bs**—Try harder.
>   **Mostly Cs**—You're a good friend.

Avoiding Gossip

There are some things, however, that aren't worth your time or attention. For example, do you know someone who loves to gossip? This person always seems to know what's going on with people—such as who just broke up, who is dating whom, what happened at the dance over the weekend, and more. She also likes to spread what she knows—or thinks she knows—to anyone who will listen.

Some teens tell this person things in confidence, maybe asking for advice. Or, they let the information slip out because they were feeling low. Imagine how hurt, upset, and angry the teens become when they learn that this person has blabbed their secrets around school.

Have you ever wondered why people gossip? It may make them feel powerful. They claim to know "secrets" that others do not know. Not all gossip is bad. Some is just sharing harmless information. But, there is another kind of gossip—the kind that hurts.

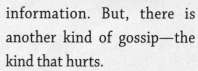

What do you do when someone tells you some gossip about another teen? Do you listen and then pass it on? Have you ever thought about how gossip affects people? The truth is that some gossip can be painful and damaging. It may even be totally false.

Malicious gossip makes the gossipers feel powerful and in control—
but it can be devastating for the victims.

Teens who gossip say:

- "You feel powerful and popular by amusing other girls with your stories, well, lies, about other girls. However it's way different when the joke is on you," says Abby.[9]

- "To be gossiped about is a gut-wrenching feeling. That's why I love to do it—my amusement, at some other girl's expense. The feeling is almighty. But afterward I sometimes feel bad," says Lindsey.[10]

One teen became upset because her friends gossiped about other teens they knew. At first she put up with it because she didn't want to argue with them about it. But, eventually she realized that these girls were bringing out the worst in her.

At that point she had a big problem. The girls didn't think they were doing anything wrong. However, the teen felt uncomfortable being around them when they gossiped. She knew that the gossip was hurting other teens. In the end, she finally found the courage to leave the group and find some different friends.[11]

> **I**f you change your thinking, you will change your life.

"Though you may gain fame and popularity at the time you're gossiping, you won't even be remembered in a few days or weeks. After graduation, your fame is over; only the pain that you gave goes on," says Hannah.[12]

Friendship

Here is some advice on what you can do if someone is spreading gossip about you:

- Confront the gossiper and deny that the gossip is true.

- Ignore it. If it is ignored or treated as if it doesn't matter, it tends to go away.

Saying Good-bye

Even among good friends who are not growing apart, relationships change. For example, one of you might have to move away. High-school seniors have to face this at graduation, after which many people may go away to college.

It can be a very exciting time in a person's life, but it can also be sad. When one senior was asked what he liked best about high school, he said he really liked getting together with a tightly knit group of friends.

He felt sad at graduation, saying, "It will be hard, being so close with a group of friends, to have everyone go their separate ways. It's hard, knowing we'll all be away . . . [from] the things we've grown up with."[13]

Even the best friendships can change when our lives change. But people can stay close throughout life if they make the effort.

Your attitude can have a huge impact on these changing relationships. Remember that you can stay in touch with friends through e-mail, social networking sites (such as Facebook), phone calls, and visiting them when you can. High-school friends can be lifelong friends. It takes work, but it's not impossible. It's all up to you to make it happen.

Friendship

Chapter Notes

Chapter 1: Friendship

1. Julia DeVillers, *GirlWise: How to Be Confident, Capable, Cool, and in Control* (New York: Three Rivers Press, 2002), p. 171.

2. Jennifer Jiggetts, "Friends Help Teens' Health, Experts Say," *Norfolk Virginian-Pilot,* January 5, 2001.

3. Ibid.

4. Ericka Lutz, *The Complete Idiot's Guide to Friendship for Teens* (Indianapolis, Ind.: Alpha, 2001), pp. 5–6.

5. Personal interview with Matt Burns, March 29, 2008.

6. Amanda Ford, *Be True to Yourself* (San Francisco: Conari Press, 2000), p. 39.

7. Julie Taylor, *The Girls' Guide to Friends* (New York: Three Rivers Press, 2002), p. 56.

8. Catherine Dee, ed., *The Girls' Book of Friendship* (Boston: Little, Brown and Company, 2001), p. 156.

9. Taylor, p. 17.

10. Ibid., p. 24.

11. Neil I. Bernstein, *How to Keep Your Teenager Out of Trouble* (New York: Workman Publishing, 2001), p. 277.

12. Kimberly Kirberger, *On Friendship: Book for Teenagers* (Deerfield Beach, Fla.: Health Communications, Inc., 2000), p. 60.

13. Taylor, p. 32.

14. Lutz, pp. 41–42.

15. Ibid., p. 45.

16. Bill Beausay, *Teenage Boys!* (Colorado Springs, Colo.: Waterbrook Press, 2001), p. 186.

17. Marlin S. Potash and Laura Potash Fruitman, *Am I Weird or Is This Normal?* (New York: Simon & Schuster, 2001), p. 185.

18. Jiggetts.

19. Lutz, p. 127.

20. Taylor, p. 159.

21. Sean Covey, *The 7 Habits of Highly Effective Teens* (New York: Simon & Schuster, 1998), p. 80.

22. Kirberger, p. 61.

Chapter 2: Popularity

1. Meg Cabot, "How to be Popular (for the Right Reasons)," *Parade.com,* August 6, 2006, <http://www.parade.com/ articles/editions/2006/edition_08-06-2006/Popular> (May 13, 2011).

2. Elizabeth Agnvall, "The Price of Popularity," *Washington Post,* May 24, 2005.

3. Jennifer Lach, "In the Mind of the Beholder," *American Demographics,* May 1, 2000.

4. Miki Simonds, "Behind the Popularity Screen," *Lancaster (PA) Intelligencer Journal*, March 3, 2007.

5. Sara Eisen, "Life as the Friend of a Man Magnet: Revisiting Sixteen," *WholeFamily.com,* n.d., <http://www.wholefamily. com/aboutteensnow/relationships_peers/crushes_and_ dating/man_magnet.html> (May 13, 2011).

6. Amanda Ford, *Be True to Yourself* (San Francisco: Conari Press, 2000), p. 159.

7. Erika V. Shearin Karres, *Mean Chicks, Cliques, and Dirty Tricks* (Avon, Mass.: Adams Media, 2004), p. 12.

8. Ibid., p. 8.

9. Ford, p. 146.

10. Miranda Hitti, "The Price of Teen Popularity," *WebMD.com*, May 17, 2005, <http://www.webmd.com/news/20050517/price-of-teen-popularity> (May 13, 2011).

11. Kimberly Kirberger, *On Friendship: Book for Teenagers* (Deerfield Beach, Fla.: Health Communications, Inc., 2000), p. 8.

12. Ibid., pp. 9–11.

13. Catherine Dee, ed., *The Girls' Book of Friendship* (Boston: Little, Brown and Company, 2001), p. 158.

14. Ford, p. 120.

15. Howard Yuan, "Discovering True Popularity," *Institute for Youth Development*, 2004, <http://www.youthdevelopment.org/articles/tn109901.htm> (May 13, 2011).

16. Gina Roberts-Grey, "Making the "A" List," *Family.com*, n.d., <http://www.teenagerstoday.com/articles/general/making-the-a-list-924/4/> (May 13. 2011).

17. Kirberger, p. 155.

18. Marlin S. Potash and Laura Potash Fruitman, *Am I Weird or Is This Normal?* (New York: Simon & Schuster, 2001), p. 135.

19. Karres, p. 69.

20. Sean Covey, *The 7 Habits of Highly Effective Teens* (New York: Simon & Schuster, 1998), p. 80.

21. Cabot.

Chapter 3: Cliques

1. Rosalind Wiseman, *Queen Bees & Wannabees* (New York: Crown Publishers, 2002), p. 19.

2. Peter Grier, "Peers as Collective Parent: In the Age of the Busy Parent, Teens Often Set Rules for Teens—on Fashion, Dating, Drug Use," *Christian Science Monitor,* April 24, 2000.

3. Amanda Ford, *Be True to Yourself* (San Francisco: Conari Press, 2000), p. 18.

4. Grier.

5. Marjorie Coeyman, "Schools Eye Social Life (High-school Students Maintain That Cliques Are Important Part of Life)," *Christian Science Monitor,* June 1, 1999.

6. Faygie Levy, "Bully for Them? Girls, Especially, Battle Cliques in Schools," *Jewish Exponent,* June 20, 2002.

7. Ibid.

8. Wiseman, p. 20.

9. Derek Chan, "Friendship and Fitting In," *Palo Alto Medical Foundation,* n.d., <http://www.pamf.org/teen/byteens/friendship.html> (May 13, 2011).

10. Coeyman.

11. Ibid.

12. Levy.

13. Anastasia Goodstein, *Totally Wired* (New York: St. Martin's Griffin, 2007), p. 79.

14. Charlene C. Giannetti and Margaret Sagarese, *Cliques* (New York: Broadway Books, 2001), p. 65.

15. Goodstein, p. 76.

16. Coeyman.

17. Erika V. Shearin Karres, *Mean Chicks, Cliques, and Dirty Tricks* (Avon, Mass.: Adams Media, 2004), p. 115.

18. Coeyman.

19. Sunita Perumpral, Betsy Graves, and James Wimmer, "We Clique Because We Click," *Roanoke Times & World News,* November 19, 2003.

20. Ibid.

21. Ibid.

22. Ibid.

23. Ibid.

24. Coeyman.

Chapter 4: Online Friendships and Communication

1. Cate T. Corcoran, "Online, Teens Flirt, Dish and Shop," *Woman's Wear Daily,* November 17, 2005.

2. Ibid.

3. "Teens Set New Rules in the Age of Social Media," *PR Newswire,* October 31, 2006.

4. Selena Ricks, "Casting a Wide 'Net'; Instant Messaging Is Expanding Teens' Circles of Friends Like Never Before, Circles That Often Include Friends Who Have Never Met Face-to-face," *Portland (MN) Press Herald,* November 10, 2003.

5. Ibid.

6. Ibid.

7. Ibid.

8. Anastasia Goodstein, *Totally Wired* (New York: St. Martin's Griffin, 2007), p. 20.

9. Julie Taylor, *The Girls' Guide to Friends* (New York: Three Rivers Press, 2002), p. 76.

10. Marcelene Edwards, "Teenagers Use Internet as Resource Tool, Means of Communication," *Knight Ridder/Tribune Business News,* June 22, 2001.

11. Ricks.

12. Ibid.

13. Ibid.

14. Amanda Lenhart and Mary Madden, "55% of Online Teens Use Social Networks and 55% Have Created Online Profiles; Older Girls Predominate," *Pew Internet & American Life Project,* January 7, 2007, <http://www.pewinternet.org/Press-Releases/2007/55-of-online-teens-use-social-networks-and-55-have-created-online-profilesolder-girls-predominate.aspx> (May 13, 2011).

15. Goodstein, p. 64.

16. Yuki Noguchi, "In Teens' Web World, MySpace Is So Last Year," *Washington Post,* October 29, 2006, <http://www.washingtonpost.com/wp-dyn/content/article/2006/10/28/AR2006102800803.html> (May 13, 2011).

17. Ibid.

18. Ibid.

19. Ibid.

20. Graeme Dickson, "Making Friends on MySpace Soapbox Soapbox," *Sunday Herald (London),* October 7, 2007.

21. Elizabeth Armstrong, "Fellowship of the Online Gamers," *Christian Science Monitor,* July 15, 2003.

22. Ibid.

Friendship

23. Pew Internet & American Life Project.

24. Taylor, p. 29.

Chapter 5: Making Friends

1. Donna Dale Carnegie, *How to Win Friends and Influence People for Teen Girls* (New York: A Fireside Book, 2005), p. 74.

2. Ibid., p. 82.

3. Ibid., p. 69.

4. Ibid., p. 66.

5. Marlin S. Potash and Laura Potash Fruitman, *Am I Weird or Is This Normal?* (New York: Simon & Schuster, 2001), p. 236.

6. Kimberly Kirberger, *On Friendship: Book for Teenagers* (Deerfield Beach, Fla.: Health Communications, Inc., 2000), p. 122.

7. Carnegie, pp. 84–85.

8. Potash and Fruitman, p. 175.

9. Ron Herron and Val J. Peter, *A Good Friend: How to Make One, How to Be One* (Boys Town, Neb.: Boys Town Press, 1998), p. 6.

10. Julia DeVillers, *GirlWise: How to Be Confident, Capable, Cool, and in Control* (New York: Three Rivers Press, 2002), p. 159.

11. Ibid.

12. Potash and Fruitman, p. 176.

13. Ericka Lutz, *The Complete Idiot's Guide to Friendship for Teens* (Indianapolis, Ind.: Alpha, 2001), p. 16.

Chapter 6: Teen Guys and Girls

1. Donna Dale Carnegie, *How to Win Friends and Influence People for Teen Girls* (New York: A Fireside Book, 2005), p. 74.

2. Catherine Dee, ed., *The Girls' Book of Friendship* (Boston: Little, Brown and Company, 2001), p. 185.

3. "Nationwide Survey Finds 80 Percent of Teenage Girls Attend All-Female Get Togethers and Slumber Parties," *PR Newswire*, November 5, 2002.

4. Marlin S. Potash and Laura Potash Fruitman, *Am I Weird or Is This Normal?* (New York: Simon & Schuster, 2001), p. 43.

5. Charlene C. Giannetti and Margaret Sagarese, *Cliques* (New York: Broadway Books, 2001), pp. 44–45.

6. Dee, pp. 162–163.

7. Julie Taylor, *The Girls' Guide to Friends* (New York: Three Rivers Press, 2002), p. 22.

8. Ericka Lutz, *The Complete Idiot's Guide to Friendship for Teens* (Indianapolis, Ind.: Alpha, 2001), p. 68.

9. Ibid., p. 69.

10. Ibid., p. 71.

11. Ibid., p. 65.

12. Bill Beausay, *Teenage Boys!* (Colorado Springs, Colo.: Waterbrook Press, 1984), p. 65.

13. Lutz, p. 73.

14. Ron Herron and Val J. Peter, *Who's in the Mirror? Finding the Real Me* (Boys Town, Neb.: Boys Town Press, 1998), p. 124.

15. Kimberly Kirberger, *On Friendship: Book for Teenagers* (Deerfield Beach, Fla.: Health Communications, Inc., 2000), p. 206.

Chapter 7: Attitude

1. Donna Dale Carnegie, *How to Win Friends and Influence People for Teen Girls* (New York: A Fireside Book, 2005), p. 36.

2. Erika V. Shearin Karres, *Mean Chicks, Cliques, and Dirty Tricks* (Avon, Mass.: Adams Media, 2004), pp. 130–131.

3. Sean Covey, *The 7 Habits of Highly Effective Teens* (New York: Simon & Schuster, 1998), p. 16.

4. Ibid., p. 17.

5. Kimberly Kirberger, *On Friendship: Book for Teenagers* (Deerfield Beach, Fla.: Health Communications, Inc., 2000), p. 318.

6. Ibid., p. 37.

7. Carnegie, p. 91.

8. Ericka Lutz, *The Complete Idiot's Guide to Friendship for Teens* (Indianapolis, Ind.: Alpha, 2001), p. 32.

9. Karres, p. 21.

10. Ibid.

11. Amanda Ford, *Be True to Yourself* (San Francisco: Conari Press, 2000), p. 69.

12. Karres, p. 35.

13. Paul Locher, "Orrville Teen Says Key to School Is Friends," *Wooster (OH) Daily Record,* January 29, 2007, <http://www.the-daily-record.com/news/article/1534211> (May 16, 2011).

aggressor—A person who starts a fight.

blog—Short for Weblog; online journal.

clique—A small group of people who are friendly only with one another and have little to do with outsiders.

hierarchy—A system of higher and lower positions of power and rank.

infatuation—A shallow, obsessive type of love.

intimidation—The act of making someone afraid.

manipulate—To manage or control in a clever way.

niche—A place or position for which a person is very well suited.

repercussions—An effect of or reaction to some event or action.

snob—A person who thinks that people who have money and a high social position are more important than those who don't have them.

stereotype—A way of thinking about a person or group that pays no attention to individual differences.

Further Reading

Amblard, Odile. *Friends Forever? Why Your Friendships Are So Important*. New York: Amulet Books, 2008.

Burningham, Sarah O'Leary. *Boyology: A Teen Girl's Crash Course in All Things Boy*. San Francisco, Calif.: Chronicle Books, 2009.

Desetta, Al, ed. *The Courage to Be Yourself: True Stories by Teens About Cliques, Conflicts, and Overcoming Peer Pressure*. Minneapolis, Minn.: Free Spirit Publishing, 2005.

Hantman, Clea. *30 Days to Finding and Keeping Sassy Sidekicks and BFFs: A Friendship Field Guide*. New York: Delacorte Press, 2009.

Internet Addresses

TeensHealth
<http://kidshealth.org/teen/>

Palo Alto Medical Foundation: Teen Emotions and Life
<http://www.pamf.org/teen/life/>

Index

A

accepting changes, 106–108
appearance, popularity and, 23, 34–35
arguments, 18–19
attitude
    accepting changes, 106–108
    "can-do," 103
    changing your mind, 103–105
    determined, 101–102
    good choices, making, 20–21, 30, 100–101
    gossip, 110–113
    listening, importance of, 108
    overview, 99–100
    quiz, 109
    saying good-bye, 113–114
attractiveness, 23

B

best friends, 13–15
Be True to Yourself (Ford), 10
blogging, 56–58
body language, 67–69, 71, 93–94
breaking up online, 56
buddy lists, 53
bullies, 44–46, 102–103

C

Carey, Mariah, 34
changing your mind, 103–105
clashes, preventing, 93
cliques
    bullies in, 44–46
    downsides of, 40–41
    female, 39–40
    joining, motivations for, 41–42
    leaving, 46–48
    outgrowing, 50
    overview, 38–39
    stereotypes and, 49–50
communication
    differences, physiological reasons for, 86–87
    facial expression, body language in, 67–69, 93–94
    female reactions, 83–85
    friends-only relationships, 88–95
    listening, importance of, 108
    male reactions, 85–86
    male *vs.* female, 82–83
    online (*see* online friendships)
    phone usage, 88
    skills, 70–72
crowds, 20–21, 24–25
cyberbullying, 45

D

dating, 95–98
decision-making skills, 50
disappointments, dealing with, 19, 35

E

e-mail, 63–65
EverQuest, 62
exercise, 35
extracurricular activities, 25

F

Facebook, 59–61
facial expressions, 67–69, 93–94
Ford, Amanda, 10
friendship
  benefits of, 7–10, 15, 17, 81
  choosing, 20–21
  online (*see* online friendships)
  outgrowing, 16–17, 42, 50, 106–108
  psychological importance of, 8–9
  romance effects on, 89, 92–93, 98
  tips on being, 18, 19, 70–72, 76, 89, 97
  variety in, 10–12
friends-only relationships, 88–95

G

Gates, Bill, 40
gay couples, 96
geeks, nerds, 40
getting along (people skills), 23
good choices, making, 20–21, 30, 100–101
good friends, 12–13
gossip, 110–113

H

happiness, 21, 30
hormones, 86

I

identities (personalities), 54–55, 60
infatuation, 97
insecurity, 28–29, 31–33
instant messaging (IM), 53, 55–56
Internet. *see also* online friendships
  addiction, 55
  overview, 51–54
  safety guidelines, 63, 65

J

jealousy, 92–93
journals, 105

L

labels, 49–50
Lady Gaga, 34
listening, importance of, 108
loneliness, 42–44

M

Madonna, 34
making friends
  communication skills, 70–72
  expressing yourself, 76–78
  finding, 73–74
  meeting people, 69–70
  new/old, 75
  new students, 72, 74–75, 104–105
  overview, 66–67
  party fears, 79–81
  shyness, 78–79
  smiling in, 67–69
maturation differences, 86
meeting people, 69–70
message boards, 59

misjudgment, 28–29

MMORPGs (massively multi-player online role-playing games), 62–63

MySpace, 59–61

N

new students, 72, 74–75, 104–105

O

online friendships
blogging, 56–58
e-mail, 63–65
games, 62–63
instant messaging (IM), 53, 55–56
message boards, 59
overview, 51–54
personalities (identities), 54–55, 60
posting statistics, 63
social networking sites, 59–62

P

party fears, 79–81

peer pressure, 20–21, 29–31, 100. *see also* cliques

personalities (identities), 54–55, 60

popularity
appearance and, 23, 34–35
characteristics of, 23–27
limitations of, 30–32
overview, 22

R

reality television, 60

rejection, 27–29, 40–41

relationships with parents, 24

risky behaviors, 30, 32

S

saying good-bye, 113–114

self-acceptance, 35–37

shyness, 78–79

smiling, 67–69

snobbishness, 27

social anxiety, 79–81

socialization differences, 86

social networking sites, 59–62

sports, 35

stereotypes, 49–50

Students Against Drunk Driving (SADD), 32

T

teasing, 45, 101–102

texting, 88

trust, 66–67

Twitter, 62

V

visualization techniques, 79–81

W

wrong crowd, 20–21, 30